KNOW
Thyself the
Knowledge
Within *You*

RICHARD JOHNSON

Printed in the United States of America

ISBN 978-1-64133-700-7 (sc)
ISBN 978-1-64133-701-4 (hc)
ISBN 978-1-64133-702-1 (e)

Library of Congress Control Number: 2026900683

2026.01.29

MainSpring Books
5901 W. Century Blvd
Suite 750
Los Angeles, CA, US, 90045

www.mainspringbooks.com

This is a photo of me with my ex-wife and my son.

Contents

Part 1

Being Neutral

This is my apostrophe on the outside going in, everything that I say is based upon truth, concrete proof, of what happened to me, in my exclamation how, I explain what transpired how' the gangs, and theTexas Syndicate, Latin kings, crips, and bloods, S & M gangs, all these things took effect, In the hatred of them hating on individuals from the state of Texas, in the year of 1994. when I entered my first two years and a half later I have made things totally different they don't single us out, and hating on Texans no more after that, most of all couldn't have done anything without the lord Al Yachwshuah and it's only change from hating Texas inmates, too the type of charge of crime you were sentence with, and for the skin color are who can get the most conjugal visits, and bring in the most Chiva in the Penta, the most ever green Gaydo or who can you control to bring in your source, of money. And for record all these dates I give in my autobiography and times when something that happened that was very critical, were changed to protect individuals from getting hurt by me RJ writing these true stores of my life true events that transpired in prison and also to give knowledge and wisdom and light and guidance to lots of young black males or even Hispanics, locked up and be told by different peoples, different gangsters and other sects, of people trying to get them to do things, when they need to listen to them hearts, and listen to the knowledge of the person that has the power that is in you. I Richard Johnson was going through a separation with my wife and didn't want to see no other man raise my child left Houston, Texas in the year of 08/09/1989 and went back to Albuquerque, New Mexico. In Houston I was working at Budget rent a car as security put in for a transfer to the Bank at 4th and Roma Sunwest Bank, in Albuquerque N.M. The paperwork of my transfer, didn't arrive there until two months later, so, I had to reside into a Motel, on center Ave, to preserve my money. I went to Noonday centers, Salvation army, homeless shelters to eat for free met an old G' by the name of Mr. Al telling me your money is not going to last you long out here! As he came towards me, I noticed he had a radio on his shoulder, with a Kango hat, color psychedelic listening to the music of Al Green saying, let me show you how to get your hustle on. Mr. Al grabbed this can extend it, in front of CVS Market and pass out, these homeless newspapers, I told him I can't do this man; I never did nothing like this I've always worked for a living. He told me how much money do you have on you. I said, $55 Mr. Al said, how long do you think that's going to last until your job call you. I took the can form Mr. Al and stood in front of CVS Marketplace people begin to pass by putting dollars bills into the can and didn't want homeless newspapers a women came by name

2

Deanna, she introduced herself, seem to be very nice saying, what a handsome guy like you doing out here? you don't look homeless to me. I tried to say I'm not I'm just only, but Al told me the money man! don't blow our cover, then she won't give. She works as a full-time tutor for Del Norte school Deanna gave me a ball up piece of paper with her phone number and address in it saying call me or drop by. I said, sure all shapes and colors of people of different ages passing by after 7 hours standing in front of the CVS Marketplace, we had $165 we left, went back to the Motel bought pizza he bought a little booze and kick back, and watched TV and plan for the next day, weeks past same old thing now I'm standing in front of the CVS Marketplace, at the entrance front door, my manager Jeff Peterson of Guardsmark Sunwest Bank sees me, and say Chwsh what are you doing out here! your paperwork has arrived, we haven't seen you in weeks get over to the office, and I'll give you a room to Lodge inside Sunwest Bank until you able to get on your feet, and get apartment, after a few weeks' checks. Jeff my manager demand for me to get in the car, I said, Mr. Jeff but as I turned to the side, I seen Mr. Al' saying, where are you going with our can, the money! I was too ashamed and embarrassed to explain to my manager Jeff what was happening, and that I made a mistake and taking the can and set down in his van as we drove off. Mr. Al ran after the van but we were a little bit too fast we already dissolved in the wind. Me and my manager arrived at the Sunwest Bank he had a room for me to stay inside the Bank, until I could get more paychecks to get a place on my own. One incident took place that ended my stay at Sunwest Bank, a little earlier, while securing the entire floors going through every room every area, checking all secured locations. One day I decided to check the inside of the vault where money is rolled on pallets and drawers fireproof files. I looked at a $1,000 dollar bill, decided to take the thousand-dollar bill and start rubbing it underneath my arms and underneath my butt, and as though I was washing myself completely, just playing around with a little humor! The second thing I noticed, a person standing outside the Bank building walking looking for some shed or covering, to get out of the cold weather and rain. then I noticed who he was it was Mr. Al I quickly open the door, and said, what are you doing out there? He came running to the door and I let Al' inside only in the Lobby area of the Bank. Mr. Al fell asleep and I let him out at, 5 in the morning. when I came to work for 12:00 noon to Sunwest, bank my manager Jeff said, Richard' I want to see you in the conference room now! Jeff and also stated to me is there anything you need to talk to me about, I said, no sir' are you sure! One of the highest executive Managers pushed a button on the video watching me take a $1,000 dollar bill rubbing it up my butt my face, my legs my body and everyone burst out laughing then he showed me the second video of Mr. Al sleeping on the sofa in the Lobby. Jeff my manager stated do you know how many people would impersonate Mr. Al, to sleep on the floor, or just on the couch, are to be a janitor? Everybody would do anything, to be lying there with a gun, and wake up and rob this Bank. Hey! Richard don't feel bad but I'm going to put you over at, old Albuquerque high school on center road, it is abandoned building. you're not doing anything there, but securing the property stopping kids from falling through an old, stage that had caved in, and stop homeless and transit no one aloud on the premises. After you be a good boy, I will bring you back to the Sunwest Bank building, for now this is your punishment! Finally, when I got a quiet place by myself which it winds up, being another Motel Travel Inn, I grab my suitcase and again taking my writings and literature of Hebrew Greek concordance, I begin to master the Bible reading from Genesis to Exodus Leviticus, Numbers Deuteronomy. Going through all my pamphlets of things, that I was studying, I always stated I just need much more time to master what I'm doing seem like the world is taking me away from somethings, I really want to do. And being security you do not discuss religion on your job. After working there for several months, I got transferred to Sun village apartments being security at the front gate that I got, transferred, again to a Plaza working across the street from the Del Norte High School, now, on a Friday night at the game room Plaza where a dollar movie Theater was downstairs. Upstairs was the Burlington Coat Factory, and a Game room center was present it was reported to me from one of the managers inside of Burlington Coat Factory that a large number of coats was missing and the children from Del Norte school are responsible always coming over during lunchtime to steal the coats and jackets. And only the 49er jackets they would take nothing else! will be missing. I arrived quickly through the double doors noticing a young man holding the 49ers jacket, and the manager was explaining to me that there were 25 more jackets well' the police was already on the scene and he came up to me and tried to take to jail, the little boy for trying to steal a 49er jacket from the store, I said, to the officer Branch hold up, let me speak to the young boy. And the sheriff of Bernalillo county replied, to me, you don't tell me a darn thing yes's I can if you know the rights of a private security officer, and knowing the penal code, you're on my grounds, and you cannot arrest are detained this young man unless I give you the authority" so stand back please sir! He was a young Hispanic boy, he is in 9th grade I said to him, what is your name Mijo Sanchez they call me snake! tell me the truth tell me, what happened. I' m coming from Del Norte School everybody came over about 25 of us between lunch hours and they all grab the jackets and they took off and started running through the double doors and I was left holding mine. I said, Snake' what is the purpose of taking the 49er jackets? Because that's what the 18th St. gangs use 49ers jackets. we want to move up the ladder to be a gang member but I didn't steal the jacket. I replied to snake, go sit in my office, I'll call your mom to come pick you up. Officer Branch looked at me and said the Brat is in the gang! I said no he's not at least not yet. Officer Branch stated you don't know who you playing with. Sorry I'm not going to press any charges on this young man, in here at Burlington Coat Factory the manager Mr. Stevenson is not going to press any charges on him you can go! Thank you for your services I called his mom Deanna I said ma'am your son is inside of Burlington come get him right now! The officer stayed outside the store passing by over and over again trying to get my attention, but I left I went to the game room then I went to the dollar Cinema, and stood there while people entering the dollar Theater. After 8:30 p.m. I was walking, to my car from the Plaza sheriff car creeped up, really slowly and as his window begin to roll down, he came to complete stop on my right side and stated to me smart ass you're right isn't nothing I can do. If I was your age I would love to give you a couple of hits across your face. But I can give you a ticket for parking in the handicap, just because your private security that doesn't mean you can disobey the rules sign this, please! I left going home to Motel Travel Inn, money was flowing so good now, I can now get right into an apartment. But I didn't I met a man that had a duplex apartment he allowed me to stay and work for free for rent and build the duplex into a one bedroom 101, landlord Michael Federoff on Anderson Street. At this time my morale was at an all-time high but begin to get low self-esteem was at its edge. I went out on center to wiener schnitzel I seen a familiar face at the flea market I met several times there ask her is she doing anything yes but only oral sex, I said sure! The time was between 6:30 Ish I got out of my car went to the passenger side and open the door for her to get in 30ft from the corner seeing a dark skin male goes by the name of Ellen Marvin Marquis, instructing her on what to do as I close the door, she hopped into the passenger side I walked around to the driver side and got in as I was driving to a location I kept seeing a car in my rear-view mirror, I asked Tammy do you know of anyone that's following us I see a car behind us, she said, no I don't see nobody" after I made two left, two turns and two rights and circle back and I parked my vehicle behind a store I asked Tammy, do you feel comfortable or do we need to go to a Motel she said, no I'm fine! Then I took out my wallet and place the money on the dash $30, she was performing oral but noticing she was also digging underneath my seat, my stash of extra cash was all on the floor, with her having the right hand with a mace bottle in it and her left hand on me jacking me off my seats were lean back to the floor as I looked up and noticed Tammy was no longer giving me oral but rubbing me with her left, hand and jacking me off holding a mace bottle in her right hand coming up, slowly reaching all the way towards my face I grab the mace bottle out, of her right hand flipped it to the side, and told her assume your position you got paid for your services your money is on the dash and you're stealing money from underneath my seat Tammy just kept looking from left to right, going down left to right, going up left to right she agreed taking off her clothes to have sex my security uniform was place in the back of the seat where she laid on top of it, before she laid down, she asked me what is this? I said, read the cap Guard smart Security' she said oh! Okay, after we finish, I drove her back to Center a block away from the wiener schnitzel fast food restaurant where I picked her up, we talked for at least 35 minutes are you going to come back around and see me? I said, sure but we going to have to get you a job and get you away from this area, where your pimp won't follow you; I know he's is my good protection from idiots that's out here on the streets. I gave Tammy promises that I was for sure going to keep she hug me and kiss me while sitting on my lap, with the door open, Tammy asked me when are you coming back, I will be here in about 5 days later I was at Milton's restaurant that's on Center Road eating dinner about 6;35 p.m. Three men came to the door one pointed at me and said outside you right now! young black male had showed me a gun that was in his belt, the other male appears to be a young white male along with a baseball bat in his right hand, and the last one had unscrewed the license plate, and put it on top of my car, looking at me through the glass window. I made a phone call to Albuquerque Police Department they arrive within 5 minutes gave him my statement and they told me to leave; I left and went to work. There was another incident that occurred while I was cruising in my Rx7 near an area called Tomball the war zone. I saw a friend that was there standing near the street corner we have already kicked it in the Traveling Inn Motel, having fun watching TV but this time she's near the street, as though she's looking for someone I pulled to the side and said, girl what you doing out here? Hey RJ get out of here right now! No, you get in, let me holler at you. this is the wrong area wrong people and and later she agreed of hopping in we drove through an alley and made a left then, a right in front of her apartment. She had told me, wait I'll be right back then a man came out and came up to the door and stated hey' she will be out in a minutes! as I was waiting there, for about 10 minutes it was very dark only one telephone post out in the middle of parking lot and for the light around the apartments I got out my car, and went over back to the door, to see what's taking so long about time I arrived to the door it was propped left open by 1 and half feet with a person standing in the direction of the door. I said, to that person hey is she still here! As I got a funny feeling around me, saying run, run, run I started bagging backwards away from the door, I speed up trying to make it to my car pulling my key ring around my finger, three gentlemen walked up to me and said we want the money! And at the same time, they hit me, I got hit with a brick on my head I fell down someone had pick me! by my right leg shaking me over and over again until my wallet fell out my security badge was still pinned to my little billfold, they looked at it and yelled out! 5, 0 let's go! I got beat up, pretty bad didn't know where my car was my keys was still around my finger luckily wearing it through the keyhole with one key bent, but I knew my car was right on the side of me. but I just couldn't see my car or put the bent key inside the keyhole. Finally made it to my feet to barely stand up when I got in, I locked the doors barely can see while driving I drove into the middle concrete bedding in the middle of the street central Ave a sheriff seen me, and pulled me over, and said I know exactly what you been doing; you like to get the heck kicked out of you, going into that neighborhood, called the war zone, let's go down to Tomball Precinct and get your statement there and get you out of here! Hey do you remember me officer" Branch Wow! That's amazing how karma always come back to bad intentions. I reckon if I would've put hands on you, still have been looking pretty I'm too old I couldn't have done as good of a job as they did! Only thugs can do it like that and who is the gentleman that pick you up, by one leg, I think you said, goes by the name of Mad dog, and started shaking you like Popeye the sailor man. I said, Sir' I never told you that; I guess you were already watching, officer Branch said enough I'm sorry I do apologize let's get down to business you already got your medicine by the way; Mr. Johnson do you need to go to the hospital? I said, no sir Mr. Branch said fine! Then he said tell me why did they take off running? could you tell me that? Why would they drop you and take off and run like a bat out of hell! That is the weirdest thing I've ever seen before, he kept questioning me who did this! I wouldn't say anything so officer Branch set me up, he told me we'll go back in the room when I went back in the room, there was one of the persons that gave me an ass kicking, his name was AJ Houston, but I didn't say anything to officer Branch I told him there's no comment I was in the wrong, I'm out of here! Six months later I received a phone call from detective Arbogast of Bernalillo wanted me to come down within 3 weeks to answered a few allegations brought against me. Six months later I met a black woman by the name of Tojanna Stevens stayed in Albuquerque Mexico location Tomball Street, in apartment 4611 we frequently met 3 to 4 times going places then finally, haven't seen her in two months later on she was in desperate need of money. We went driving in Albuquerque locations and pass by Milton's cafe and ate inside the restaurant afterwards I was driving she ask me to pull over and we started kissing having sexual intercourse I noticed, that it was a foul smell I cut on my light and noticed that she was on her ministration got mad at her told her to get out the car, where I threw the seat covers out the car along with that was wet from her, was thrown out the window. Along with money that was given to her later I told her while having a tool in my hand lecturing Tojanna of what she should not have done while on her time of the month. verbally disrespecting her, but told her Hey! no problem, I will bring you back home go ahead and get back in, I drove Tojanna back up to her apartment area, and asked her is there anything else you need she said, no I'm sorry I should've told you and I said, yes that would have been a whole lot better but hey it's all good.

Part 2

Transgressions Multiplied

My wickedness begins to be manifested of the transgressions that I begin to do. feeling lonely away from my wife, noticing that now I am feeling urges, within me that have never felt before I begin to have more female acquaintance. In 1990 1 year after I arrived back to Albuquerque, N.M. Also, I met a man by the name of Laurence Hearns he needed a place to stay he only had a car, and I helped Mr. Laurence out, by giving him a place to stay in the Motel, also teaching him Hebrew, and knowing that the Bible is actually a black point of view. Mr. Laurence was between 42 years of age and I was 28 years' old and I said, you mean to tell me, out of all this time from your childhood to growing up as a man, you have never known that the image of God is our skin color? Laurence said, no I was always told that his skin was white person white is clean black is dirty, black is evil' I said, no Mr. Laurence black is beautiful! That's why you going through your persecutions right now because everything of the matrix on the flip side of the underworld is all against you, do you need any melanin, in your skin to work out in extreme heat and in the sun, our bodies automatically produce. White people need melanin, in their skin so the beautiful flesh with the perfect flesh of the original of black skin was the only way of survival of heat of 165 in biblical aspect had you also seen the movie called Mandingo? He got shot and from the rifle blast, fell backwards and was shoved with a pitch fork in his chest and pushed into the boiling pot. Yes! Laurence stated; that was awful we talked for hours day after day but later, on we had a confrontation" because I was smoking green herbs and I told Mr. Laurence, while I was smoking green herbs, he's telling me that I'm allowing the herbs to take control of my character! And he felt that I wasn't being fair about it, but just being disrespectful and that wasn't quite right; because I had a women friend that worked at the Baptist hospital in Album, N.M. 1523 Joel Road, as a receptionist, that was smoking along with me her name Charlene she was laughing, and I was laughing also we heard a knock on the door, and it was Mr. Laurence was just coming to the room and we already been there for hours he has interrupted me and Charlene, by laying down and watching us as we were steady smoking ain't y'all a little bit too loud over there? And where all this disrespect comes from? And I said, to Mr. Laurence seem like you got enough money to take care of your own self, or why don't you just go ahead, and leave, Lawrence left the motel we still stayed as friends seeing each other every now, and then I would pass by the Noonday centers and the God's kitchen, just to help out, and pass out food and groceries to the people that was in need remembering that I was once homeless, and without a job. I kept writing back to the 1928 Delaware my address, but mom never answered returned to the sender. There was one person would not let me forget that I was once homeless, Mr. Al walk past me with his radio on his shoulder, and his psychedelic Kangol hat, on his head singing the song of Al Green, call me call me, what a beautiful time we had together. He always gives me the guilt trip, like I should have never separated, I should have stayed being homeless along with him. I love you my friend you taught me the game of hustling with a can. But not enough to be homeless get a job! Then I walked away, also I kept in touch, with my ex-wife Lorraine sending money to her as often as she needed for my son Rayk-e. But then lost contact with her feeling lonely, and depressed, and begin to date another escort in 1990 one year prior to the time, of the first prostitute. There was one person named Henrietta Begay she helps give sermons at her church, she always inviting me, I met her at the flea market she told me she worked at Peachtree clothing store on center road avenue. Ms. Begay was Navajo precious person believing in Jesus we talk scriptures all the time and as often when I pass by her store, we were talking about the image of God, but nobody wants to talk about the image of God and explaining to her about the flipside. And asking Begay have you ever seen the cartoon the flipside she said, yes, all the time I think it was a nice cartoon or what do you think about religion flipside? What is white it's truly black and what is really black actually white. What do you mean? Tell me what do you mean, by that give me more input. The Lord was whooped 37/ slashes, if you done your history and you knew the rights and the Laws and regulations of the Roman colony no one could be whooped if anyone was a Roman and if he was whooped, that person will be put on a slow cooking fire. But now the Roman skin would bleed and not stop. Their skin was free bleeders at that time the blood and plasma has not even been discover yet in the world also no one had designed the blood transfusion, so therefore if they get cut they bleed to death, and unless they take the flesh off a servant, or slave, and cut it from the servant and put it on to the Roman skin and branded the skin with a hot iron. Xena the warrior Goddess showed some documentation on exactly that we talk for hours and later her friend at work name Marie added, to the conversation and why was apostle Paul cornered in the Antonio castle of Jerusalem, in the alley way of the wall of petition. Why didn't know one cross to go over to get Paul they just tried to grab his arm and rip him apart. Just pulling on both sizes left arm to the right arm. Also, later on that week detective Arbogast, called me in for questioning at the station he felt, that he had no grounds to hold me left the case on hold, for one year then link the first case to the second recent case. The female name Tojanna Stevenson in 08/25/1991 I was indicted within 90 days stayed in county 3 weeks, I was in my cell before going to my trial. I pleaded with yachwshuah please! If you turn this from me and I don't go to prison I will be a new man I said, test me, please! Test my spirit to see if I will do exactly what you tell me to do. In seconds the yachwshuah test me I sat on the toilet, to use the restroom a correctional officer came knocking on my door banging with his fist saying to me, trial date! get off the toilet right now, drop what you're doing and let's go. I said, to the correctional officer, man" are you playing with me? Are you kidding me? Then at least allowed me to wipe my ass in the process the officer said one more time get off the toilet right now and let's go to court. Then I replied will you shut your mouth. I will get off the toilet when I wipe my ass and finish what I'm doing! then it dawned on me that the yachwshuah sent a correctional officer over to my cell that fast to test me to see if I would hold me patience and be calm and have a positive reply. I failed my test; I must face this time and do exactly what he tells me to do. I was in jail for 16 months before sentencing I had a court appointed Attorney Greg Worley. I had a trial by jury, with two people walked out and one of them said which was a woman, my son was in the same predicament I don't need to be here! she stated and the man said he was here for a rape case not to make a decision upon consensual sex. the jury bent backwards and it was on the third day of deliberations as they brought me out of court, and into the cell the first time with two guards standing outside of my cell telling me it looks really good' you doing an excellent job.   Now it was time to go back up, but when I went up to the Judge; before I entered the Judge chamber, I heard the receptionist talking to the Judge stating that they threaten to punch her in the eyes and also said, that they are refusing to come up with a verdict. Unless he signed something as they see me standing in the doorway, with the two guards on the side of me he said to me, come into his chamber, along with the receptionist. Richard Blackhurst said, to me you already admitted what you said you did! Now you need to sign your signature on this piece of paper. I looked at Greg Worley my Attorney and said, do I have to sign this paper? You have to or they will throw the book at you Greg Worley said to me sign it" I ask for a cup of water as the water was place towards me the handcuffs was loosen where I can sign the piece of paper, and after I sign on a piece of yellow paper, I was grabbing the water with my left hand, and quickly, they grab my hand back from my glass of water, that was handed to me, and handcuffed me back, with my hands handcuffed behind my back. Brought me back down to the cell as I kept yelling out loud, I won't my water! I won't my glass of water! I was shoved into a cell again, sitting in a five by seven saying to myself, what's going on? What the hell did I do? Bodyguards they're been with me for the whole duration of three days told me you're about the dumbest person I've ever met in my entire life. that was an Allen charge! A shotgun order! He didn't supposed to enter the chamber" and you sign, that you did do your crime so therefore they will take the piece of paper to the Jury and now the Jury must come up, with a verdict guilty as charged. I hollered like a straight fool but to no avail what's done! What's signed. Before the Judge Richard Blackhurst read the verdict, he said there was once upon a time when a man had sinned, we would say sin no more. But that's not how I do things then he hit the hammer on the desk for 221/2 years sentence 1994 at the first month of the 12th day waiting to be taken to grants Correctional facility for the valuation you know" just remembering I had a chance of getting out, and posting bail before I went to court. A friend named Henrietta Bagay came to see me along with a man by the name of Elmer Aragon in the county jail. I ask her can she get my last check from my job? She replied yes, I can do that for whatever it's worth. I told her I didn't want to sell my Rx 7 car to post bond but she convinced me that was the only way she could get enough money to post bond. After I sign the car title, I never heard from her again. They purified me as gold tried in the fires, and I got a chance to talk to the number one top hot shot; Attorney the best by the name of Mary Hine's and I explain the whole story to her, she said messing with those whores on the street huh! Richard, I know both females and I know they are prostitutes, why didn't you call me earlier? You could've given me, the car that would have been close enough because I'm going to need at least $10,000 besides Henrietta and Elmer Aragon, the world is looking for them, by the way you are 997 miles away from your destination. congratulations! Richard, you got had! high price to pay for a piece of p*****! I was speechless as yeast in dough my wickedness was multiplied and it was finally, magnified two of the females was putting false accusations on me and I had the money to bail out, but I was tricked by a Preacher and a Prophetess. Well on this rape case I stayed in the county jail, for 18 months in the county jail, G" pod second floor, I always had a saying when it's time to man up to me responsibilities poise like Michael, feet plant like Janet, I got the Pac ka Feary make my enemies hear me, let me rule like the hog the boss for what it cost! And exit the correctional facility with no losses who is this coming from Edom with his robes red as crimson perfect my ways oh! Malach, I stayed there for the remainder of the time until I was given the sentence by the court we had two Bunks for two inmates to a room. my roommate's name was William Jimenez I had a problem with William one of my believed to be first friends, he was my roommate we talked about the word of the lord, I showed him books after books documentation of historical events and he always shook his head as though he believe me. But when it came for him to tell me how he felt he told me, do you remember someone told Paul? I will say to you chews! Your long studying has bothered your brain, and I don't believe any words you said. And I said, you just now telling me this! William stated yes's chews you never asked me Two weeks later I had a friend there named Paul a white man. And a Mexican man by the name of Roberto Albert, secondly, he was my closest friend there! Roberto come from old Mexico he stated that his wife put false accusations against him and their children lied, and his wife was trying to make the children believe that whatever transpired did happen. Now they have to expedite him back to old Mexico from Albuquerque New Mexico. while he's waiting, he's residing in the Bernalillo County jail at B.C.D.C finding out what happen to him I gave him knowledge that all his charges will be dropped and they were. Because at time he didn't believe that his charges would be dropped. Roberto felt that he was going to be locked up for over 30 years. We prayed every day and gave thanks to the Lord yachwshuah. Roberto was always talking to me about the spirit of truth, who we are before we come to earth. One day he told me he was in a deep vision and was dreaming, but in the vision as though Roberto was given by someone high above the earth. And was inside a huge boat, and he could not look at the person face, but Roberto was in the boat. For about the first 3 weeks of meeting him, he kept letting me know all about it. I was getting a little annoyed I didn't know how to respond to what he stated and I did believe him, but not all what Roberto saying was adding up. Until then I had two visions the first one, was that I was watching two people having sexual intercourse with this vision was giving me a Cat scan or a radar of a giant vagina and a man's private going in and out in and out nothing sexual. It was like an actual body of heat ray sensor showing me and watching it 3-D as I said, what is this! And then an arrow pointed at the image and it magnified just as big as a giant Globe. And it scared me But I knew what the vision was telling me; it was showing me that I had aids and I pray to the Lord yachwshuah, I said, take this away from me please! And the yachwshuah said, I will, because of this you will receive pain and suffering as a reminder. I woke up, quickly form my first vision and try to forget that vision ever happen. The Lord knows that I did not want to remember that vision and then I went back to sleep for the next vision or visions within so many more very hard to count them. But this one, I was in a boat high above the stars of the earth. Looking at a person that looks like my friend actually, it was Roberto, as I tried to look in front of him the person that one of heavenly quash meaning? Most holy one" was sitting directly in front of us. I was not allowed to actually see his power of radiance, then I heard a voice said, get out, I didn't understand why, but he said, to get out now as we both went down in the clouds, we wind up going into an ocean, then a tunnel inside of the ocean leading to dry ground of a Giant cave. as I was walking through a presence was with me, but my friend Roberto was gone, I could not find him and as

I seen some kind of sparkle of a light startled me, for the color is like the true colors" is where all the original colors come from. So I took off running and it gave me light where I could see as I turned to the right, and I made another right, then I turned to the left, I went through a narrow entrance of a hole of a cave and I started walking through that narrow spot came out towards a cliff gazing downwards seem to be a women arrayed in reddish armor speaking on a plateau like if it lead up to steps and millions upon millions of whoever they are the so-called holy ones that have fallen in taking in by the world. We were all hit by a timely aftermath of apocrypha genocide of fleshly genetics of angelic, beings shape shifters surround her watching listening to her as she has a Giant audience and I heard her say, that no one can stop us, we are imperial to anyone's attacks we will demolished the earth, in no time' then someone on the right side of me shown out with a goldish brownish and then turn to silver, as it was turning into a white light, colors among colors but only one entity and he is Yahushua of the righteous they seen it, the angelic being came running after me, because he is my source of Eternal true presence of my light; they came running up the walls of the Giant cave, and her presents carried her as though she flew. I ran taking a left, taking a right, running as fast as I could but she caught up with me and walking towards me in front of me and said, who are you I was amazed to see holes within her skin, as though her skin is not really her flesh. and I told her you know who I am eternal all-seeing eyes of the seven menorahs of the genocide gene of the Most Holy Markab of the seven Malachy I am of the Adama yachwshuah who you! And all others can't defeat I woke up, quickly' and ran to Roberto and before I could explain anything to Roberto a presence came as I was reaching out to touch hands as an agreement the presence lasted for about 30 seconds it was like a magnetic field of strengthening power, of a presence tingling all over our bodies Roberto said do you feel it; yes! I feel it, from my feet to my face. cleansing" I said, then Roberto said, now can you help me understand the vision now, yes, my friend I saw you on the boat with me in the vision I believe you. So, I gave Roberto my knowledge of interpretation of what his vision and extent was and he felt right because he knew it was righteous and he said it was good but now for the first vision of my interpretation as we walked over to the TV everyone is watching the news and then a news break! Emergency broadcast interrupted and said we have a breaking news report a women died today of full-blown aids they showed a picture of women. I recognize that women I got up from the table, and walk straight to the room everyone looking at me in a wonder and Roberto came to my room and said, what's going on I said, call the paramedics, I knew what my vision was about pain and suffering two shots in my hip's infirmary medical showed up to G pod and asked me do you want me to take you out for a checkup for aids? Yet! How do you know you have it? you have been in here for 16 months I said give me my shots and let me go on by my business. I'm not giving you a shot until I check you out. I got to draw blood from you I replied then draw the blood and do what it takes to get this stuff out of me please! Two hours later the doctor ran back to G pod and stated; how in the hell do you know that's impossible" well come get your shots now and by the way you don't have aids you have a high number of syphilis even a famous stars died of this Al Capone undetectable in the blood no one should have known this after that day was finish three weeks later" I had another vision of a women with a child by herself walking holding the infant her face was not recognizable but later her face started to look familiar with long black hair white female crying out for help and then I woke up next day I was talking to a friend name Anthony Steele's, history on his character he's a bible thumper loves scripture was married but he had also a stepdaughter not his biological daughter but all he stated was he remembered was entering the house and she's laying down in a pool of blood Anthony woke up, next to her and don't remember what happened I won't make no comment. Now, my 4th friend named Paul was praying every day and was a strong believer he always wanted to master the scriptures and read them like me; the spirit of the lord was with Paul he got knowledgeable in the scriptures he listened and he study all the time. I used to listen to him read the first book of Peter two Chapters by heart. But something happened with him that evening from the weeks we studied a new county inmate, came in and Paul went across to H pod while we stayed in G pod. Paul went across to H pod to talk to this person, and this person was claiming to be a he, she" Navajo Indian goes by the name Niah every morning Paul would go to the H pod, instead of being with me and studying with the rest of us, and praying. Paul begins to be emotionally attached as if it was his girlfriend, finally he begs Henry the correction officer working our floor, to give him a few hours, of time together and the C O said alright" I'm going to turn my head for a couple of hours, somehow word got back, that Paul had sexual relations with that Niah. Paul became distant wasn't talking anymore to me or to anyone and fellow shipping with the Lord. One week prior to that time as I was hearing gashes of hits, beatings like' if somebody is getting hit by somebody else! We all search every room besides Paul room; I ran into the room of Paul and as I entered I heard Paul say stop it! Chews stop it! that hurts; I looked at Paul in his eyes watching him, bleed from his mouth and head. I looked directly in his eyes that is not me, I don't know what's happening with you, and before I understood it' his arms begin to twist as though someone pulling him face, forward down with both of his hands turning them inside out, as Paul jerked up, finally an inmate called out, to Henry C O and he, called the paramedics, and call correctional officers as they running towards the room, they notice Paul was pushing, shoving himself from one side to the other, as though he is getting shoved by something or someone. They put Paul in a strait jacket, and took him to the infirmary two days later Paul, came back and he's okay' talking as he was laying down on the weight bench just looking towards Niah cell, as he set up and got off the bench and walked towards the H pod, Paul went back into convulsions as though he was, catching a seizure foaming at the mouth, eyes went behind his sockets, they brought him to another floor, A pod the handicapped, and been there ever since. Then there was another incident that occur with a person by the name of Chaves he's the S N M crew at the Albuquerque County Jail B.C.D.C. Chaves been on TV awfully a lot, speaking out for little children not to be like him, being a known gangster for 25 years in 1993 Chaves managed to break out of the county jail him and four of his boys they managed to overpower one of the guards of P pod, tied him up, and took his walkie radio, put an apple in his month, and duct taped him. Took the weight bench and threw it through the glass window, tied six sheets, together to calm down 200 ft high the first inmate swing down, on the sheet going back and forth until he manage to skip his feet lunged on to the concrete, and then he finish sliding down the wall before hitting the concrete floor, but ran into five guards that beat the hell out, of him. The next one swing down on a sheet named Turbo swinging back and forth as he swings, everybody' you can hear them, that was watching saying go, go go, Turbo thought he made it across, but got stuck on the bob wire on the fence. But he was able to get out of that and then got tacked by a women correctional officer. The other two got down and escaped, hopped into a vehicle change clothes, and got caught walking around two weeks in their boxers, my time is drawing near, after getting sentenced 22 1/2 to Santa Fe Correctional facility, in 1994 Grants is the actual evaluation facility, you stay there before going to the Santa Fe main facility, for the Lord have said to me I have given you a Greek and Hebrew concordance at B C D C county jail through the hands of a correctional officer" Henry on the third floor, for after the break out we no longer stayed on the second floor. we got move to the third floor, because of Chaves break out changed everything. Now' listen to my wisdom! And the Lord told me you will master every single thing that's in this concordance. And you don't have one now' but you will be given another one to have and keep it, wherever you go. And about that time when you stated that you had said one day; you needed more time to master my work you have plenty of time now' go do what I told you to do before and I obeyed the Lord but made one comment" saying yeah about time I get in there to do your work the correctional officers are the Warden will take it away from me my Hebrew and Greek concordance and yachwshuah also said when you get to Grants for evaluation ask sister Sarah to write a letter from the bishop there to grant you for the literature never be taken away. Again, if by any means it's taking away from you it will come back to you always just as it was given to you also remember" the vision of the Band in the books of the Scrolls that you stood before obey it when Al yachwshuah had finish talking. I was praying on my knees within seconds a person which is a correctional officer came up, to me and said this belong to you this is yours, I know you can use this, and that's how I received my second Hebrew & Greek concordance again, I also was spending much time on the Egyptian Hieroglyphs of understanding what the names truly mean. For example let me give you Moses name, by the hieroglyphics ThwThmashash in Hebrew signs of the time, of signs of the mighty fire, of fire (Th- signs -w- of time Th-sign Ma- mighty- Sh-fire a-sh -upon fire) this name existed over thousands of years way before the book of Moses was actually wrote. I say, that is a lot of food to eat as well' and to learn all about. Now in reading the documentation on Joseph Smith mastering his notes, and writings and learning that he was the only one trying to show that the Egyptians was actually the sons of Abraham. Arriving from Grants to Santa Fe Correctional Facility the main 6/08/1994. The prison had an underground floor for Inmates, for orientation for the new Inmates entering Santa Fe, most newcomers had to stay there for at least a week before being place to General Population or particular Pod or Level, I watched Inmates that were veterans been down 20 plus years came down to the stairs, and stated to everyone if you are a P.C. Case you can't be here! What are your charges? Baby raper's you better be at the PNM north unit locked up. after they came down to talk to us, and give us a warning said to us in orientation, remember Inmate's process all every person coming in, and also going out we give you clothes to wear, hygiene toothpaste then the veterans went back upstairs. several Inmates that came with me went to protective custody P.C. voluntarily seg because of their crimes done against children also the veterans stated that we know your charges we knew your charges before you came here months ago, so don't try to lie to us. when the next day pass 11:30 a.m. Normally Orientation would eat together but this time all of us was let out to go upstairs straight to chow hall as I sat with my friends and in a group of Spanish Inmates with my tray getting ready to eat a black group of Islamic stood up and said come over here! I noticed they was pointing towards me so I said, who are you talking about? Islamic guy said you're the only black person over there! So, I told my friends that I have to leave and go over to sit and eat before long I seen an officer come up and say what are you trying to do start a race riot. As I walked over to the Islamic militant characters stating to me, you must be a fish you don't sit with Mexicans you don't sit with Spanish you sit with your own kind. And let me find out you're a Texas boy' and living anywhere in the state of Texas. hearing these words of hating on Texas, and fish" I was pissed he could be my first dish as a lion scratch his itch; transforming into the Norm, nuts bigger than king Kong started my scriptures in heart I got up couldn't eat no more left the chow hall went to the correctional chapel a pastor by the name of father Dennis goes by the name of rabbi black he heard me speaking to plenty of the inmates out of the church and told me that he would love to hear and talk to me on the black nation that is in the Bible and told me that anything I need documents in his Library take it as it's yours for the taking my Library is yours, and don't have to call me father Dennis please! Complete this book and we have discussions on this many times with many Inmates, and Correctional Facility letting them know that I am doing a revision on the Bible mostly the OT, father Dennis always recorded as we talked inside his chapel. One morning after I entered the weight room, I was approached by a large male Aaron hood, by the name of Big Red while I was bench pressing 225 which I could not lift up, already took it off the rack, I looked to my left, there was a man laying down and someone dropped a 75 lb. weight curl, on his head at the same time I was trying to pump 225 lb., Big Red came above me, to help me lift and spotting me, saying Pump it, pump it I said, hey! Who in hell is you, well' anyways make yourself useful, pull it up! When I see the man skull get crushed through, I was able to lift it four times. Noticing the Lord has put the favor, with me to allowing the Aaron Hood to protect me being a witness Big Red Kok gang leader" he said don't be in the interrogation room, no more than 5 minutes I was out the office within 3 minutes going back to my destination you get kudos for not snitching, also most of all you get to live. I left walking back to my pod, couldn't but notice as I was approaching my room hearing inmate crying out' that hurts, that hurts, over and over again then someone yelled out, then get up and fight don't you believe in the Lord turn your butt checks, hearing one of the Syndicate gang members said, why everybody that believe in Jesus

Christ always come to prison and be Saints and preachers knowing that they are Chesters and molesters' baby rapers, now tell me we're they Preachers on the outside, molesting little boys at the same time and five-year-old girls. Later on, that day as I was walking outside to recreation before going out we ate lunch called brunch I was eating bacon and eggs and sausage and toast I went back for seconds serve, arriving back to my seat, it was already taken by inmate. I was sitting at a different seat and the Muslim told me don't eat bacon at my table. I told the Muslim I've been in the county Jail for 18 months I haven't taste bacon and real bacon as that" since the free world Muslim stated I'm tell you again you don't eat bacon at my table I proceeded to stuff the bacon in my month he threw his arms down and punched the iron table with his fist saying, do you offend Allah? Excuse me sir! That Jello that you're eating right now! That is pig guts and hog grinds sugar and dye to add to your glucose and pork everyone in the state of Texas knows that Jello is fat, a form of pork then Eman Muslim said to me, I know this guy is not from the state of Texas, is he? saying that at the same time he pointed towards me to his crowd around him. I said, to him so tell me? you don't like Slim Thug from Texas, how about DJ screw, 2Pac, Al Green then he said to me and to everyone around us. If Chews is from H-Town he's a dead man and his music he listens to of these guys from H-town or unless he converts and the guys wear a skirt and crying that it hurts when I heard the comment he made I wanted to get at this so call Eman but I knew it was too many of them called the family" I was outnumbered such ashamed black on black crime exist behind bars as well in the streets. I will pray to Al yachwshuah quash keep me within his grips of not transforming into the African hero a straight, Negro on his ass. Just to cool off I left to go outside for recreation to play basketball. we are playing three on three Tournaments the winner gets a six pack of any kind of Soda water" me, Anthony Shorts and Daniel Lacy, playing against AJ Houston, T Mack, and George Lacy, his nephew everyone was watching me because they the defending team couldn't stop me I kept going straight to the rim laying the ball up, shooting all over them doing the Harlem Globetrotters backwards they couldn't stop it they were very angry and mads that's where I met AJ for the second time and he could not stop the reversal or anything finally AJ made a comment" saying to me, that's why I hit you in the head with a brick you couldn't be stopped. Later on, he came back up and told me he apologizes it's squashed that was a cheap shot! Sorry good win! I asked him, a quick question? how is it, that your name is AJ Houston. he said, Chwsh! please! don't feel like fighting with these fools, they don't like my name or anyone from Housing T, and don't say the rapper Z-ro I said, gotcha" when we played the best out of three games we won and the winners get a case of sodas, I gave mine to AJ I didn't drink sodas but they felt that I got moist out, by doing that which I should've taken it and not giving it out so quickly. They made lots of comments that Texas man got hops and fast the end of the day after I got through playing basketball coming in from recreation by myself, sweating and hot, tried I looked inside the metal ice chest I was digging for ice to put in my water' I saw Seagram wine coolers and mickeys at the bottom of the chest. Sanchez and all his boys told me not to dig too far, in the ice. Again, I looked at the Seagram wine coolers and mickey's and I said, to myself I'm not a drinker but for all these years I definitely can take one of those mickeys as the metal doors opened for me to enter A-5 Pod, I ignored my eyes and didn't get any water and walk through the gate first floor A-5 Pod, going up stairs to B-5 Pod, room 137 while walking up, all the Texas Syndicate said, you made a wise choice! wise decision! That's ours the Correctional officers owed us so they bring it to us every week. Watching two of the officers walking in front of two Inmates and stuffing two knives in both of their pockets talking noise to them saying you need to get out of here! Right now, before I take you to Hard lock up! But also supplying knives I felt very bad, I said to myself if the Correctional officers obey the Texas Syndicate and give them knives Seagram wine coolers I'm through I'm good as dead. One morning at the main facility I went by the law library where a man by the name of Robert More called one eye" as soon as I walk up to his desk, he salutes me with the Arabic As-Salami, Alaykum so I said to him with the same salute of greetings so you telling me I need to pay you $30 to start working on my case while I'm in here, but at the same time, you going to turn my case over to the essay, slang for Mexicans, no brother I can't do that' one eye stated to me illegal to do so nobody can't do that; I said, anybody can do that we all in the penitentiary. One eye said, so you don't want me to work on your case" no sir" not at all I could do me own thank you very much. Another thing one eye, said before you leave keep your religion to yourself nobody wants to hear that about your white king, are your white Bible and I told him, beside keep your Muhammad to yourself it started 570 A.D. And ended in 632 A.D. What are you talking about? I spoke to one eye that is the starting of Mohammad boy called wolf throwing rocks into a cave it cracked bust open a vase where the Scrolls that he used to write the Documentation came from the dead sea Scrolls named after the Quran cave. I didn't know that" are you coming out on the yard and talk to me about this nope! you might have your boys out there for me. He smiled and stood up and said you're a very smart brother" I said, but not smart enough I'm in here! Let me give you a little advice thing has been set in order before you got here, what the family Planning on doing to Housing T, has nothing to do with you. Don't let the ones of the family of 67 know what's in your brain keep the Texas stuff, H Town music the Boss, Z-Ro down on the low don't let nobody know you're listening to this music and that you are from the same location and state of Texas, now is there any way I can hear some more of this I said, seems like you need to listen to a little Z-Ro yourself everyday same things sure just call on the name of the Texas brother Chwsh and I will come and represent, one eye said, I find it very offensive for you to keep telling me about Texas when I told you I don't like with Texas H-Town boys and I stated to him I find it very offensive for you to salute me with the Arabic greeting! And you have no knowledge of what you are greeting me with. Then one eye said what are you talking about? I've been studying Arabic and being Muslim for over 28 years, who are you to tell me this you can't be no more than 30 years old. I give you that you're close, but try 31 also said to him, let's break your Arabic name down and see what it really means As- meaning fire salami – the fire of God one nation Alaykum – one God he is the truth of our people. Then one eye looked at me face to face and said, do it say that in this white man's book yes but is not a white man book it is a black man book remembering history if you read the Autobiography of Malcolm X he stated that Elijah Mohammed prayed looking into the Bible with tears of agony and soul he knew that there was a key to opening the book but he had not the key so he did not read the book. well," I have the key and knowledge is key and it's all above Al yachwshuah then one eye stated to me why do you keep saying that name. I said I think it's fair to say this is my first time saying the name in front of you, yes" but others have stated that you've been mentioning this name. I said, let me see you are a black male age at least 48 years old and you have never heard of the name Chews. One eye said yes's I've heard of that name but you put a yak before" you say, Chwsh and I said, you are correct ya- is I am chwsh true fire- The A' always goes where is a letter even though you don't see it, the letter A' is always there so you put it before the (ch -w-sh) of kinsmen – ah so chwsh is your nationality not Asiatic black male or Afro American. Then one eye proceeded to raise both hands and say this is a lot deeper than actually anyone could think of. I have never known those things; I better get out of here before someone sees that I am converting so do you believe your doctrine is irrefutable no wonder you win converts. look Chwsh I apologize! I know I am of the family group, and I can't stop what they are about to do and how they choose to do it. I can voice my own opinion from here forth I would not claim you in anyway as an enemy hopefully we will meet again on a different circumstance stay strong brother you are correct. I will have to start back to looking at what I'm studying I'll get back with you on this topic. One afternoon I met an Inmate by the name of Jeffery Epps he was in pod 3, close to the orientation above the deck not downstairs. he asked me did I know any pointers to help him, get out loop holes to overturn the decision he been sentence to 564 years of which he already had done 12 at this straight. The information I gave him was to look up his case, go back to his Attorney and see if he can get the entire docketing statement to where he can find loop holes and he did they never read him his rights but it was very difficult to prove so he been doing time trying to file a motion of limine, meaning a formal request asking the Judge to rule on the admissibility of certain evidence, before

KNOW THYSELF THE KNOWLEDGE WITHIN YOU

it is presented to the jury. And to get back in court this way! He can at least reduce his sentence by 2 to 3 years to were instead of 564 years he has 365. thank you chwsh, he replied about time you see me again; I will have this reduce again, all these jail house lawyers that's all I needed to know. I will keep going back to the same Judge to re-evaluate. Thanks I really appreciate it everything I'm hearing about you is the real deal. Weeks later, I was in my cell Texas Syndicate Sanchez came up first time meeting him, and Sanchez was telling me, who are you? where are you from? I said from the state of Texas whoa" don't say that too loud. your looks, seem to be different than most black men, yes, I am, I said, then Sanchez replied are you in a gang? No I'm not! No gang, or you a crip, no I'm not no crip! Blood no blood, no Muslim" are you Islamic nope I'm not Israelite hey, I think you're running out of religions. Ok Sanchez said, how about the family group? No I'm not part of that group at all. Well I'm through questioning you, for now all I can tell you is stay out of our business and stay out of what we do and you'll be okay. That's not quite so simple for me to do that you're Rollin blacks up! Left and right burning them out of their cell shanking 2 to 3 a week. It's only a matter time before me and you will collide! Yes, Sanchez said that might be so but remember I fight against Chester's child molesters including rapist of all kinds and trying to control the Chiva is hell with people around here it's my area and this is what I do! And this Earl Mayfield cooks the dope and spreads it and you can bet every last bit of these so-called religious Inmates are Chester's rapist but they want to be popes and Preachers inside Santa Fe correctional facility you're right I have a problem with that! And just to let you know, if you get jacked up by correction officers and put in certain office doesn't spend no more than 5 minutes and get the out of there! Chwsh I will talk to you later" you seem to be a good person that's why I gave you input between this, it is what I do. Later that night Sanchez came back up to me and stated listen I don't know if you familiar with the family group they are already giving me your info, the charges brought against you what lead you to prison and believe it or not you really don't have charges we already know both men that were pimping the two girls that got sexual penetration charges one was 19 years old and the other was 21 years old chwsh you were 29 years old high price to pay for a piece of P*** and the Eman wants us to handle business hopefully that will push you directly to the family. I said, to Sanchez hold up! Wait! Do you know how we, become a member of the family group? No! Yes! I think so, no Sanchez that's not good enough" do you know what they do? no Chwsh I don't any black male that wants to be part of the family group must kill two essays so you see you're helping the Eman whoever he wants to be part of the group, but you didn't know why your boys are disappearing two by two someone always have an arterial motive yes Sanchez said but I can't believe you didn't jump at that" it was the best time to join the group why didn't you? I said, I'm guided by the Automatic pilot of righteousness yachwshuah governs my heart for a justification and a cause! And I fight freely no strings attached, no wicked plans behind no arterial motive. Ok time will tell if you do have a righteous cause or not, I'm out of here talk to you later Chwsh.

Part 3

Not Acknowledging Leadership is Persecutions

E arly at 4:45 a.m. Cells doors opening up, sound like a freight train letting go cabooses click! clock! click! It is wise to be on point, salute! When the cells doors open watching both sides of the room. When afternoon lunch came, I went out on the complex into general population as soon as I went through the metal detectors, two people approached me and said man you look like a guy that caused a riot here name Al Kapone his real name is Richard Johnson that goes by the same name! you have kinfolk I smiled and kept walking and said nope I'm not. Now there was two different clicks that try to rule the black males behind bars Islamic and Muslim they were flagging me to stop and to talk to several individuals he was Muslim name Leonard sitting down on top of the wooden bench beside him was a man Robert more they call him one eye! Mainly" because he only has one eye. Who wanted me to come back to talk with him, some more about Hebrew Robert was sitting at the table left side of him asking me are you down with us? I asked him with whom" then his friend which is next to him the Eman of Muslim name M. Leonard said, to me you know well! What I'm talking about then one eye over talked Leonard and said, this is a good brother let's look at somebody else! But Leonard said no! I'm not he's going to learn and don't say not a word we know all about your crime! you did to get here! Now are you down with us or not. And I'm assuming that is a yes "so if you are down with us, there are two things you must do to be part of this rule of the black family. you must kill two essays you don't have a choice, not yours that will prove that you are one of us. And by the way you have been talking about our Plans on Housing T, this was already in motion before you got here! and it well happen. Can't stop us so again leave it, along sit back and watch handle your two essays show us, that you are one of us, and that you're not a snitch and one other thing! you can't get out of this family group and you can't leave the family and I replied no! I'm not, and I mean no disrespect' I came in here by myself and I will leave going out by myself! the Eman of Muslim insisted I'm give you time to think about it after the day was over with several Islamic and also Muslim guys was asking me, why are you teaching a white man's book? I am trying to explain to the Muslims that this is not a white man's book it's a black man's book. Then he said I see you converting 8 to 9 people into this white man's religion do you want me to call out all their names? I have a problem with that" Robert said Hey! Can we make a man be part of our family? Leonard said see! what I mean" sounds like you're being converted already remember no one leaves the family' understand that! So you can hit fast as lightning huh! Hey' I don't want no troubles! Well looks like you got trouble! I walked quickly away from where we were located near the wooden bench around the jogging track walking straight through the metal detectors back to the double doors to go through the hall to get back to the Pod 5-B top floor, I arrived back to my cell and as soon as I got back to my cell four individuals came and approach me and started fighting one hit me saying I got the Thugs in his face! The other person kicks me and said while kicking me, what you said Z-Ro? as I caught the leg push him on the floor, I hit the other person woke up underneath the toilet with water dropping in my face. The person standing over, said, I liked Lil Keke but I didn't know you were from Housing T, also told me quit listening to that H Town music and put on the kufi hat for Islamic well I fell back on to the floor, couldn't see good at all bad sight. I realized, that they have taken my Hebrew and Greek concordance and all my books of 17 of the bibles that I have written alone with a button picture of my son Rayk-e my wife Lorraine and me. I got up from the floor, approach a person by the name of Earl Mayfield he had his side kick a man by the name of New York that sell dope along with him, helping Mayfield out, a devious person hates to speak about the despicable things he would do, taking advantage of Earl and everyone else! in the control of Chiva nevertheless Earl he cooks dope for the inmates inside penitentiary and sells it! to the essays. while I was walking towards his cell Earl said, hey! Man" sorry what happened to you and them I listen to Snoop Dogg, I listen to Z-Ro I live in H-Town they don't tell me a thing. But of course I can't play the music in general population it will be terror but, I said, of course you cook dope there's a big reason why they don't mess with you, slip up! And don't make none! yeah you are correct" Mayfield stated he also told me, don't go to war yet, let me see if I can put the squeeze on them Man" look at your face, the five of them got you really bad brother" I said, five of them? It was four of then he said, nope I'm positive it was five the other one was Eddie Ray goes by the name of big country. I' ma see by not giving them no dope to anyone in this Penitentiary. Between the time before the two days came New York would make essays bow down to him and make them suck his private and disgraced them and talk bad to them, he knew that they were not going to do anything because they were hooked to chive. apparently, it was never mentioned to Mayfield what New York was doing. After 2 days Mayfield told me to quit staying in the room get out, so the person has a chance to put back to what was taken away. But nothing came up, Earl was more frustrated he said to me I should at least got your picture back of your child and your wife any you. I said, to him what about my other literature and my Bible my notes, don't do anything yet wait for me, Earl said, I waited for a day first thing in the morning he was able to give me my picture of my son Rayk-e, my wife and me that button pin on also king James Bible. but nothing else! I knew that if I didn't fight back or do anything, somebody else! Is coming for me, so I said yes! I will wear the kufi hat showing that I have changed and being converted over to Islam so I put it on for show! Quickly left the area grab the knives out of the windows of the top pier, from my room of the top edge of the window. I grab them, cross back to my room. Sled both knives in each underarm deodorant. wrap and taped around them having two of them one in my right hand, one in my left hand took off the kufi hat from my head and swung it down like a frisbee to the first floor, of the bottom pier. I left back inside my cell and waited patiently until I seen one person that was responsible for the way my face looked like the hellraisers. he was coming back from recreation so I took my hair down which I had a huge Afro took my double hair down which was on my chin. I've braided my chin sat on the side of the individual. And he didn't know who I was. Left him for a moment then took a knee and bowed and prayed to Ala yachwshuah you are most quash. If able! To be my choice to choose my king I will wear your suit before I wear the suit of the serpent and you my Lord do not bow the knee to no fleshly man or worldly creation of wicked hands that has not the righteousness in his heart and don't walk upright, then I grab someone's boom box" sitting on the edge of the cell and played the music the boss so everyone will know it was me chwsh that turn the music on and with the help of Adama yachwshuah from this time forth I will rule like a boss and exit with no losses. I went back to him and sat on the side of Mason he said, you look just like the one just got his Z Th K, ass whooped! I am, that one then, cut him by his lower abdomen and cutting again on the other side of his arm after he pushed away screaming, then Mason Boyer begs please!! don't kill me please! And I said, number one we didn't have to go this far! chwsh please! Man! Let me tell you something! just give me a chance to say what you don't know? I said, what do I not understand about your family group they are the B F L black family leaders and the 67 member's killers of all gangs everyone will hurt, they're plan on arriving to Housing T, within six months or less, they are a new gang here! They want to get those rapper's that why really" you got named after the ones they want to get. all of this because you wanted me to change my perspective and be in your religion. And number two because I'm H-Town bound! Number three" whoever is in your religion they have to stick or kill an essay as I was speaking, he started back getting strong yelling, because his people were coming in, from recreation hearing the gate open inmates came back from general population. I jumped out, mason cell and went in front of them and looking at their faces, they were wondering where the Texas music was was coming from. With quickness I swing towards the three individuals Carlton Ray, Willie Johnson, and Deandre, before they ever knew what happened as they lie there bleeding in their cells. I'm standing over them looking down on them shouting as I went into a trance they were all double clutching balled into a knot laying on the floor holding their stomachs while I took out my right pocket and look at my picture, of me my son Rayk-e my x-wife Lorraine it was a pin on that I had from the state fair that when you take a picture they can put your picture on a pin clip to a button we can where it on our shirt. But I didn't I carried it in my pocket while I was gazing at the picture that's all I had of what family" I had that was left from the free world. But there was one who I cut, that was crawling towards me said, we will be in Housing T three weeks from now. I stared at him, then look up and spoke anybody else want some of this H-Town boy" actually I'm from BMT 89 miles away since nobody from H-Town wants their cover to be blown! Are the whole card pulled! too scared let someone know but I will represent H-Town to the fullest. I will represent before I get me was killed, all of y'all need to get away go to your cells locked down is coming! this is my doing no one had any part in this! the first time I knew that death is drawing near, thoughts are running in my head that I should've got the Eman of Muslim from the first time I met him when the Eman finds out he will send for all his boys to kill me I was angry and hot I was mad, heart beating fast tears are running down my face because I know it's time to die. In this Penitentiary rule #1 you use a knife you get stabbed by a knife yachwshuah presents came in dwelling all around me I begin to feel a wonderful presence of cum peace, power strength, my feet to my head to my whole-body tingling strengthening power just like I felt from the county jail B C D C some inmate stay out of their rooms watching me to see what's next the Lord Ala yachwshuah told me you're not fighting a battle that I have not won, trust in me you do only, for this time forth you can even trust your enemies, two Mexican men came up to me and said, give me the shank I said, no! I'm not giving the shanks to you; I will give you the shanks on the side of your neck! Sanchez said, do you not remember a young boy by the name of snake! I said, yes, he's my friend and I will go back to war for him. Snake is my little Nephew Sanchez stated now" if we wanted to harm you we can look around you. From top pier to the bottom, so many people. Then I heard a voice telling me trust your enemies then he got one of his boys to shove my Bible notes the last of what was missing, my literature 17 books of all my stuff that Mr. black the bishop gave me. Sanchez said to me now quit doubting my intentions give us the shanks both of them we don't have much time. Yachwshuah presence told me that they were not trying to hurt me they were in for the ride so I handed both shanks to him, he tells me to take off my clothes and put on his clothing saying to me chwsh get out of here! Hide your face go and you can turn the music off for now, you can put it back on later your point has been made. And they finish up working the individuals over sticking them over and over again hearing Sanchez Texas Syndicate say so you are Housing T killers I will for sure write kites in all Penitentiary to be on the lookout for B F L if the warden don't try to block my letter's I thought somebody was going to die which I didn't stay around to see if they did or not just hoping that Sanchez did what I asked him to do! make them bleed don't kill. first thing in the morning it was front-page news that essays took up for a black man. And allied with the most fearful gang in Santa Fe correctional facility immediately correctional officers lock down the entire unit came to get me and put me inside of a room 101 and tried to get me to acknowledged who did this to my face and how are you in the mix of this" and how those inmates got stabbed the officer also stated that your case has been turned over to the essays and they didn't kill you? So your own peoples have sold you out" remembering what one of the essays had told me along with a friend of Aaron hood Big Red don't stay more than 5 minutes are you will be classified as a snitch! Snitches get stitches and buried in ditches and covered with dirt by those that wear skirts and cry that it hurts, think of anything to get yourself out of that interrogation room. I started yelling at the correction officer that if he doesn't let me out of here! I was going to break somebody neck immediately I was going back to my cell where people are gathered, in Pod 5 meeting by Texas Syndicate watching as I enter my cell yelling out! What we know for sure you're not a snitch!! and definitely not from Albuquerque I said, very loudly I am from the state of Texas Housing T, H-Town quickly one of the Syndicate said, don't say that too loud inmates like knowing anything about H-Town Boys over here now I understand why the family group has been making everyone join or else! You're cool with us, but nobody from Albuquerque loves H-Town Texas boys and now we finally know why that's where the family group gang started and remember we have under covers ready to report back to Leonard here in our Pod 5 right now so keep on the low and we will find them they don't like any or wherever you at in the state of Texas I said, then looks like I'm in for plenty more fights. Sanchez said you're cool with us we accept you as you are! Then I asked him why are you called the Texas Syndicate if you don't like Texas. Chwsh it's not that I don't like Texas because I do like Texas our gang originated in Texas because we have infiltrated for years every area of prison there is not one prison that we are not in even overseas out of Texas limits we also got people still now, getting extradited everywhere in Albuquerque but undercover for whatever reasons! Also said Sanchez tells me if you got put in Dallas, Fort Worth, anywhere Houston prisons anywhere and I am sending a kite there and it will say look out for the new gang, B F

L don't let them breathe they are the undercover enemies, of everyone! Syndicate, my seal, will take care of them if I say so, and if he or she" don't someone will die in the gang of our family T Syndicate. and now in Albuquerque we are the only ones can be called by that name and you chwsh you fight for Righteousness cause, freedom fighter so for anybody ask about you it's C.F.F.R you're not crip but you looked out for them, not in the gang, but taking up for all gangs! not a blood, but you represent and talked good for Islamic and Muslim of the one called one eye. Pod meeting was over with then Sanchez had said to me stay in your cell we will bring you food because if the officers cannot see your face, like this! you'll be back in the the interrogation room for questioning again. And chwsh remember' if anyone has a problem with you, I have a problem with them" now who's on your mind for pay back list? Snake has a bone to pick with the so-called Leonard, of Muslim, Sanchez, also said, we will make sure the so call H-Town killers want make it to H-Town, to even try. I said Chwsh has it under control' but thanks okay, then let snake know I replied I will. Afterwards Sanchez brought me 12 burritos, 5 bags of chips 3 packs of smokes, which I don't smoke and brought me some nice cool drinks called hooch two brand-new warm up, suits one pair of tennis shoes then, I interrupted and stated could you switch out one of the warm up suits for the Seagram wine coolers, I seen in the ice Sanchez reply sure I can do that! Sanchez asked me what do you have to do with father Dannis? Rabbi black" I said we talk over Hebrew and literature of the Bible. tell me more! I don't understand what do you have to do with him? I'm writing the books in Hebrew. what the books of the Bible? Yes, Sanchez came and sat down in my cell and close the door and said, please tell me I started off by saying there's a lot of things in the Bible that we could uncover but people choose not to understand. Tell me one' In the Book of Matthew the three wise men came from the East they called them Magy well! Actually three, but the truth there were seven kings came from the East but the three stayed near Jesus' birth they were Mexican black Jews originally magician's powerful wizards they had so much power it was Believe that they could rain down fire and brimstone upon a whole city of the world. The 12 tribes of Israel feared those men along with everyone else even king Haroldian Sanchez said, but why is it Mexican when the name would not been Mexico at that time! I said, you are correct; it would be under Media, or Persia is your genealogy history family tree, your nation is royal priesthood along with every African that is of Kamet. Sanchez stated I want to hear more of this real, good news something I needed to know a long time ago. But I will be back thanks Chwsh! Out of 83 inmates in the Pod 5, I was the only black person left there! For all the rest got them cells burnt or put on fire the S N M gang took total control and allowing me to walk as I please! For this time every black person that knew of me, but didn't know me" wish that they had my friendship knowing that I had peace. Before Sanchez left I asked him more questions. What about a friend of mine that's next-door to us in Pod 4, his name Angelo Truitt" he's a fair kind of guy we just found out that he's half black, and half Spanish speaks good Spanish lived in Mexico and language he's was bilingual. he was given information to other blacks; he was being a mediator it was believed to be he was causing hatred. But Angelo turned down Leonard offer' to join the B F L, so actually he was not, he was on his own and hated by all black people. your gang Texas Syndicate came for him because you didn't know him and he tossed up nine of your boys to where, the C O, said they will come to get Angelo out because the Syndicate would've killed him. Chwsh I really don't recall that one! then Sanke came over and said uncle! you know him" the one who took up for Terry J from H-Town. when he was jamming on the song, control by Janet. Big geese beat him down for playing Texas music. Yes, I remember now, Chwsh but for you, and for me making it right! No harm will be done to him permanently, I said, Earl Mayfield, he helped put the squeeze on the dope. Yes, and because you know him, we will let him get a chance to leave quietly but remember he sells dope he gets all my men hooked on dope he got one of my closest friends hooked on this dope. Goes by the name of super Dave, and that's the constant fight of me and Earl keeping our people addicted to this dope because most men would even turn on me, just to get their fix okay 10-4. I went back into the room to sit down and pray and thank the Lord for all the things he's giving me through the hands of inmates causes wicked hearts to be softened and keeping me in favor of righteousness and justice this quick dream I had of me, stepping over millions of fishes as I walked up a giant hill like the Sandia Crest Mountain, then in a vision seeing a giant light going around turning as it's was a Ferris wheel, of a time shining while I was standing in the middle an audience beyond my wildest dream I woke up quickly and said to myself, I know, I' am not that important! Sanke sent a word to me that the Eman of the family group has someone running his business and this person has been there undercover the whole time he stated that this person runs the track, short man everybody on the compound knows he got lots of money and when he gets out, he will be in the movies he also has actors and stars coming to visit him in the penitentiary here he runs the family group and has the final say so other than Leonard also Sanchez sent a kite to make sure that I know at any given time, I can be locked up going to the P N M north unit. He was correct, as I left the Santa Fe main facility, and was headed to the north unit. Where I was in hard seg time for 4 ½, months the catholic bishop's name father Dannis came to see me. Chwsh are you alright? Do you need anything? Yes, give me some of those Hebrew books that you've been reading, that you told me "That the scholars know of, I want to see them and look at them when? ASAP before the end of the shift father Dannis came back with all the books name it and claim it, he said, I'll give you whatever you need finish your writing than he left that morning there was a person that was doing 34 years this person was able to be B O special privileges to get up! And clean up and feed us to pass out the food trays for us to eat at chow for the correctional officers and one of the gangsters on the floor stated to him don't do that the inmate replied Man! I am tired of being in my room for over 8 to 9 years constant 30 minutes, recreation 30 minutes for a shower and now I'm down to my last two years I'm going to do this because I want to clean up. Beside you can't get out of your cell and whoop my ass anyway. So shut the hell up! ain't a thing you can do to me, you're not super Dave. The inmate put his earphones back on listening to music and mopping the floor. This was one of the reasons why the points System change in 1996 John shanks declare war on every gangster want to be. Because of the exact reason of a level six and level two put in the same area one is getting out in two years and the other having a life sentence of 500 hundred years cannot mix together somehow the S & M gang member had put a nylon string on the trigger of the latch to loosen the trigger and then pull the cell door open. I heard him, straining and hollering while he was pulling the door open. went up to the person that was mopping the floor, and hit him so hard gave him a major concussion the gang member" went back inside his cell and close the door and no correctional officer don't know, what happened they thought the young man slip and fell, and hit his head. After three months of seg I left lock up and went to a small general population that's where I met bear, one of the guys they call big country, Eddie Ray the one Earl told me there was one more B F L he was of 67 crew he was the fifth person I had a fight with but couldn't find him when the fight was on like donkey Kong! I said, are you still set in your heart! To get to Housing T and because your B F L leader wants to rob, rappers of fame and fortune! Then Eddie replied, Hey! I didn't know about all of plans! I told him is this squash with you! Or do you want to finish up, no I don't want no part of it, I'm done! Sorry Leonard forced me, look at my face, I said, and my hands was held high. Calling me hey! Z-Ro, I finally got, Slim Thug he's going down! telling me I always like Lil Keke but I didn't know there was Texas" I said no you wasn't forced you had a choice! I was wrong bear stated to cause all that as I went to my room, I noticed there were several individuals a man by the of Jalill. History on that person a "blood was at the main facility but somebody took his gold chain and he refused to fight! Jalill tried to get inmates in an up roar, and writing kites for people to take care of his responsibilities and so since he didn't want to go hand-to-hand combat with anyone but trying to get other people to fight his battle Jalill P.C went to lock down voluntarily. Everyone says that he is affiliated with a known police force undercover you would think to yourself why would a person have a cell phone in his room for over 8 months. Why! is he's having sexual intercourse with the female correctional officers" and why is he controlling all the dope chive, heron green herbs, he's always trying to buy every person coming near him. Jalill told me, I heard that you are a good warrior I need that kind of type of people around me I give you a woman to come to your visit and you can get her to bring you in some dope between her legs and nobody want find out, and if you want a phone, I get you one of those! anyways that's history on Jalill. Also there was another young man into protective custody a young blood brother name Kyle history on him is you can buy him just show him the money, he doesn't like crips he's 100% blood Kyle Allen red beanie, red shoes, red shorts, red shirts, red tear drops but you can talk to him as long as you act as a father figure still believes in the Lord but in a red point of view! All came from the main facility to the P.N.M. North unit. Jalill found out that I know how to sharpen metal and make shanks Jalill gave me one I need, this sharpen bad please! Chwsh I pay you for it, I asked Jalill who is this going to be used on whom Jalill said, nobody! It's just for my protection every day. I was sharpening up! when I finished. I learned that Kyle went to go give it to Iceman now history on Iceman crip 25 years of hardcore violence in heart, takes up and represent his own people as for anybody that needs help crip to the die! built like a black superman. Jalill tells me that Iceman heard fat Charles call him a snitch, so Jalill tells me that he told Iceman to handle that" so Iceman went out and approached fat Charles and act as though he was getting really close to him, I heard that you said, that I am a snitch, is that right? Charles replied yeah, but that's not how it happened Charles replied again I said, as Charles was explaining to Iceman got closer and stabbed him in the chest near his lung now Jalill was explaining to me what happened, then he grabbed me in a hug and then said, it's on he's already stabbing him. We were all at the P.N.M. North unit no more than 3 weeks to a month then got even worser word went out that Jalill lost a lot of dope and weed. meaning behind several correctional officers but there is only one thing! Jalill wanted so he decided to set up Leroy Torres along with Danny called Dan Dan. Because they were responsible for stabbing a blood gang member! initially started the Riot in Las Cruces which led to John Shanks General of secretary of corrections started and declared war against every gangster, every crip, every blood at every Texas Syndicate every S&M Jalill, tell me to go downstairs and see where he's at and if he's downstairs made sure that he knows to come up to get him some Chiva which is heron, as Dan Dan, took his first fix, and fell back on his bunk in the room and couldn't be moved. Leroy kept beating him in his chest beating above his heart" after 5 to 10 minutes Leroy Torres yelling wakes up! Wake up! I ran back upstairs sat in my room and start making a prayer in the name of Challa yachwshuah" Jalill asked me is he dead? Is Dan Dan dead? I said yeah for about 10 minutes what! What! Do you mean? What do you mean? Jalill stated he came back through!! he's now up and kicking Leroy pulling him back on to the bed and now he's resting Kyle Allen said, yeah, he's resting now, as for me and Kyle as soon as we started back talking about the situation, we seen Jalill grab all his belongings his mattress his books TV drag everything straight to the door and sat outside the door two correctional officers showed up in escorting him straight to P.C. Voluntarily lock up look like it was going to be a bloodbath I had to stop officers from getting killed I could not let, those shanks getting into the hands of Leroy Torres and Dan Dan after he came back to life! I went outside into the yard, walk through the metal detector went inside the maintenance room where they kept the mop buckets and slid the metal pieces that's inside the mop buckets out which someone had turned them into instruments of sharp metal, there already known as knives I took them and hid them hurried went back and forth, through the metal detector having five per shoe three times in a row, without getting caught or noticed. Walk to my Pod and came into Kyle room to let him know what I done because I didn't want him to take blame for something that I did, this would have been the worst of an evil plot riding Massacre of correctional officers they all hung out and had they're meeting inside the maintenance building 30 pieces of sharp metal pieces, inside the room well! Word went out that an inmate went to the maintenance room to take out all sharp pieces of solid steel, shanks and save the officers lives and only a few inmates could have that access to doing that" now everybody's trying to figure out who was the inmate that saved these officers lives. I rolled all the metal pieces into a black garbage bag and tied a knot and set it outside the door of the main walkway where all correctional officers can see it now my life was in danger again, I don't know what happened to Kyle Allen he disappeared went into voluntarily lock up! Once two lieutenants came up to me and said that was a good thing you did" but at the same time I don't know why this correctional officer fool! Went to population and stated loud and clear" if it wasn't for an inmate goes by the name of Chwsh! Saving my life I would have been dead, all your sorry low life y'all guys tried to kill me the officer ran his mouth. The two lieutenants told me, you're the only one that we would trust and pop the door open without handcuffs to put something inside a doorway of the main hallway that was a good thing you did we have to shipped you quickly away from here again we do apologize for this and thank you for you as an inmate cared for the life of correctional officers that will be remembered for taking all those shanks that was in the maintenance building you are very highly courageous you are truly a freedom fighter" you're not hooked to any gang! you fight, alone and I see truly death have no power over you in the flesh because definitely you are marked by every inmate if they found this out" I'm shipping you back to Las Cruces again, the correctional officer lieutenant of the P.N.M. North tells me. One more thing my friend Chwsh I did hear about you! What you did in helping stop bloodshed, and bringing all people together" to hunt down B.F.L. We are with you on that we will also search I will myself, to hunt the same one's that did this to you, until there is none! I'm old school I have weight among every Correctional officer, Central Correctional, Southern New Mexico, Las Cruces, all areas when I arrive back to Las Cruces the penitentiary has a program where inmates make license plates, wooden tables, desk wooden benches, for court houses and desk returns this is, where I meet a man by the name of Juanito Fernando he's doing over life sentence 389 years Juanito already done 17 straight years begging everybody I'll give you commissary I give you dope I will do anything if you could just put me inside of one of those desks returns and don't worry about, I get out just put me inside of it there for when the truck comes to pick up and they make their delivery I slide on out, and I'll be free. so finally super Dave convince several inmates to seal him inside the desk return with the panel that can be removed by five tack nails. So Friday afternoon the truck came they also put license plates wrap in boxes and two returns two tables and tree benches super Dave was now in the truck, and no one knew finally after four hours of searching correction officers was looking for super Dave but couldn't find him we were locked down for three days finally they found super Dave on the street walking around in his white boxers no shoes, no shirt, when he finally came out of hard lock down and back into general population of Las Cruces by the warden chuck three months past there was another situation when super Dave was on top of the roof of the special projects, we had over 40 inmates working getting paid $.85 an hour to do furniture we went out for a break super Dave the maintenance man for the top of the building cleaning all gutters and loose debris by hand in the shops where we work at. he got a chance to get on top of the roof walking near the gutters and yelling out my name! Chwsh! Chwsh! I and other inmates was turning to look up to see if the correctional officer in the high tower can see him, and what he wanted it was at this time he tells me; I got it now! I'm going to do it right this time. I said what are you talking about? you don't see it! I told super Dave see what! he said, on top of the building but I didn't see nylon rope ties, into a large tarp he proceeded to swag the nylon with a left to right arm up and down to where the tarp pulled up in the wind caught underneath it and as if you're not aware of the balloon fest in Sandia Crest Mountain the wind is just as strong in Las Cruces at this time everyone can see that he was beginning to have trouble, keeping the tarp low without going up, in the air he was trying to step on top of it, but it blew away from him and the air caught underneath the tarp again and he started floating, the nylon rope pulled and he went up the last words we all heard super Dave said, I'm not trying to go now this is the wrong time. It seems to be as he was in the air it pulled him so fast at 15 to 20 mph but the nylon rope was a little bit too long to where he hung more as he was going up everyone started saying go! Go! super Dave go super Dave go! Go! then he slams and crash straight into the bob wire fence we were all locked down for two weeks with the theory of conspiracy of inmates trying to escape. When he was the only one trying to escape it was stated that they had to cut the Bob wire from around him completely out of the fence because it sliced his leg arm, neck and body. later about 9 to 10 months it was stated that super Dave had one last try walking with a limp since he fell into the Bob wire now have a swag and he's walking in pain, but okay" there was a correctional officer that everybody on the compound knew that looked just like him so super Dave used that for his escape plan finally he didn't believe the same thing at first" Dave never seen that before but now super Dave went up to the officer and beat him, and pull him inside the control room took his radio tied the officer up! walked out into the parking lot with the officer car keys but didn't realize how to get the car on, he's been locked up for so long, to where he never seen a button push to unlock the car door and turn on the car. Cops finally caught him after five hours in the parking lot. Cameras revealed his hiding spot. After that we never seen super Dave again, for the correctional facility was in so much of embarrassment to where they hid so many things that he was doing his name became proverbial so we as inmates, would use his name as in saying" transforming into super Dave and get the hell out of this prison. Few months later as I was kicked back diligently going through my scriptures in my cell eating a ramen noodle soup cut up, with summer sausage inside along with some squeeze cheese and a little throwback of chips inside have to use my stinger to warm up! the water first. Before I throw it all in while reciting my scriptures by heart then a whole bunch of my friends came to my room asking for me, associate calls himself, half dead, was there! Colorado Alexander Pickering, better known as the voucher" was there! Daniel Lacy, AJ Houston, Tyrone white, Jeffery Epps, was the speaker telling me I remember when only you fought the whole B.F.L. Family group at Santa Fe main facility, everyone was in a state of shock of what they did to you, and what you did to them and how many flock with you to support the push all those enemies. where are they now? Housing T killers we can't find one B.F.L. I need your help Chwsh they took my girl Josie" I said, what's going on with Josie? Is your family in the free world is doing good? Josie your daughter, right? They took her Epps said, no Chwsh I'm talking about Josie my roommate the S& M gang taken her saying they want her back, telling me I didn't pay enough money for her! So far, I paid over $3,500 I told everybody that they can strap up, let's go to war I over talked, Mr. Epps by cutting him off from talking" with hand signaling hold up! By no disrespect I don't fight over butt nugget! I fight because you're the only black man in a Pod and they want to eliminate you; I fight because of your rights was violated! I fight because that's the only way around this situation, or if someone is trying to take your innocents as a manhood. Now you're telling me that you are going to war because your sexual intentions are loving a man and not a women go ahead wrap Mr. Epps up! Tape around them both, stack the books and let them go and those who choose to go with them go right ahead I would not take part of that; sorry and I'm still your friend but I'm not a dumb friend. History on Jeffery Epps the same person at Santa Fe correctional facility asked me advice about his case he has been down doing 15 straight years he had 565 years but he filed a motion to court to reduce his sentence to now he has 365 and now has reduced to 275 and he tells me I'll be out before you with time serve. It was said that he fired a rocket launcher and blew up the whole city trying to destroy the actual trailer home where his girl was cheating on him. I told him he takes a chance of putting another death sentence on rehashing his case for a murder or whatever you do in this fight! you flip-flop your dreams to be a butt nugget King! I said to him filthy dreamers, wicked ties that bind the mind. A few weeks before the actual riot took place in1996 in Las Cruces was a discussion on how many rapists and pedophiles Chesters and molesters we have on the compound in general population Sanchez tell me there's a group of black males that have baby rapist and snitches I stated to Sanchez from the first time we had this conversation in 1994 at Santa Fe correctional facility the main location we talked out the same topic and you know what? that wouldn't be close because we only have 125 black males on this compound consists of 595 the other rest is all Mexican and Spanish and if you would say one or two Asians about 165 whites which only leaves 305 which that is about approximately how many Mexican and Spanish man, we have Sanchez said, ok so what are you telling me the rumor was someone stating that it was over 200 of black males incarcerated for sex crimes dealing with child rapist pedophiles snitching whatever you want to call them. I will give you

50 and in lock up and 35 in general population. I don't need to search or ask a few Lieutenants and even the warden to give me information in order to mediate this particular cause. Now out of 305 inmates how many of them have the same crimes or even worser! Sanchez said we check everybody crimes before they inter the gang. I will give three, or four at the most maybe without our knowing we don't deal with that if we find out anyone has that kind of crime, he won't be part of our Texas Syndicate, but you couldn't prove it! And I would even not believe that" do you remember your last leader named Angel? And why he stepped down yes! I remember him. He was the only person by himself new of 4 to 5 years ago! The B F L found out how, to check with paper work on him by finding what he did long ago that was true! used it against him, by showing Texas Syndicate, so black family leaders had paper work on Angel, gave it to the new riders of Texas Syndicate, but you say no one never knew why Angel stepped down? Because he had baby raping charges and the gang found out and they made him give up, his throne and most of all he wanted to give up the gang because he seen daylight seeing these year's getting close, he wanted to get out of prison and how do I know? Because I talk to him myself, when I was in lock up! doing seg time here at Las Cruces and I was transferred too central. This should be my third time, arriving back here! To Las Cruces now you have over 270 in your gang Sanchez stated I don't like hearing that and I wish that I could see more paper work but I will do my homework and I'll get back with you on this! I said, how about I show you 10 members that you eat with every day that has the same charges. Chwsh, I believe you, I hate to say that" but you would not lie to me as I wouldn't lie to you! But I didn't know that" I will get back with you on the same conversation. In the month, 02-28-1996 one day at Las Cruces, while playing basketball an inmate sitting down on the bleaches or wooden bench. Watching us playing basketball his name Chills from Roswell a good man, and a godly fearing man" he told me keep your eyes up and look around you Chwsh! Then, Art, Samoan the gym Recreator also receiving a warning from a lieutenant Delatorre correctional officer LT. he calls me stretch "because when I'm in the air, I stretch over people that's in the way, and dunk on top of them he

said, it might be something happening inside the gym be careful. Sanchez boys quickly ran inside the gym and gave me a warning telling me come on, I got the hallway in the path clear and straight for you to get out the gym and out the gate. you and your homies let's go! While running up to me when I was playing basketball I immediately stopped and said, hey! AJ Houston, Tyrone White, Daniel Lacy, let's go as we exit the gym, I ran to the gate 300 Essays was on the left side of us breaking through the outer gate to run inside the gym where the fight was on after Chills left the bleaches other corrupt gangster starts throwing 75-pound weights while all of us were playing basketball inmates was knocked out or hit severely on the head then there was one man name Ishimoto 6ft 11 inches height 254 pounds solid oak knocking each S.N.M gang members one time! Putting them to sleep in a pile of heap! Was said that he had over 24 essays laying on top of each other and steady hitting them one time history he's from New York inciting a riot Supposedly is responsible for the killing over 18 officers in the riot, doing life sentence Correctional facility in New York in that particular year" so the warden at that penitentiary transferred him to Las Cruces, the only man that can wear a durag in the chow hall and no correctional officer tell him to take it off well Ishemoo was trapped in the gym. One man was running from the crowds that was dropping weights, and bars jumped up! And tried to grab the basketball goal but didn't realize it was breakaway rims that tilted, he hugs on the goal but they pull him down and push him on the floor and grab the weight bar and threw it through his head smashing his brains his name was J doobie a blood gang, his best friend, that was fighting near him named Joe compost turn his head while fighting and ran out of nowhere and dove on top of J doobie and grabbed his brains of what pieces remains on the floor scattered and held him close while getting kicked and punched while, still holding J doobie tightly! Also managed to put it inside of a plastic bag later' they were able to put it on ice and preserve his skull. We ran out of the gate and managed to get past the first then a Correctional officers lock the gate behind us as we were escorted to go to the chow hall. me and AJ Houston stood back-to-back standing on top of the tables ready to fight

Daniel headed straight and quickly went to Pod p and Tyrone quickly went to Pod O, for 2 hours then started running out of the door of the Chow Hall bodies was beginning to pile up as we were running a inmates name Chill's from Roswell came out of nowhere / 240 inmates can you make it to the Pod Chwsh I said, yes AJ behind me Chills from Roswell stopped all the correction officers from beating us down and running to the Pods to Ramshaw our rooms. They all supported us, and make sure that nobody didn't get beat up making sure that the Texas Syndicate didn't eliminate all black men after that Chills disappeared in the crowd and blended in with regular inmates and helicopters was above us correctional officers watching and running after us with dogs' spotlights everywhere running from every angle above the penitentiary and everybody was transferred to Dallas County Jail 1996/02/28 this brought change to the environment was the worst riot ever by these measurements taken war on crip gang, war on blood gangs, war on every kind of gangster John shanks declared at this time and the points level was revised by Particular type of inmate crime and history on file of each, individual if you had a certain number of points, he was not allowed to go to level six if you're not level six well we are now in level six also to mention that in the place of the Texas Syndicate and S N M, and remember SNM is the same for S&M gang they were all locked up! This is what happen when these two gangs come together, they wanted every black man to die! To be exterminated at Las Cruces at this time of the year" and because of this is what's happen to these gangs! John Shanks wanted war on them secretly locked up those gangs and let the Latin Kings Rome the land of Las Cruces to keep Texas Syndicate and S.&.M in checkmate "the Latin kings were given their spot done by the Secretary of state along with John Shanks now we are secretly transferred to Dallas in 1996. along with every bad boy there was one inmate super Dave! was not transferred but whoever they can think of secretly got shipped there. Also! And all TVs and radios must be clear casing no more solid black casing will be in the correctional facility that's how all the knives came through TVs and electrical radio devices came into Las Cruces 300 Spanish and Mexican men, against 15 black men that got caught inside the gym and the gate was locked.

Now at Dallas Texas County Jail down town no more than a few days being there this first happened the correctional officers open the door to other inmates on the side of us Dallas County and let them come in and mix with us. They came in and was just fine we were playing Domino's when one of the discussions took a turn for the worst quickly, Mexican and Spanish gangs when a Dallas County inmate said wherein, they get that tear drop! Hey ain't y'all from New Mexico another inmate said, hell yeah these tried to exterminate our race" they had to locked down the Pod and get all the Dallas inmates out they kept yelling war, ! war no talking, war! All the hardcore gangsters were from New Mexico wanted out! Secretly outnumbered too many blacks people everywhere! And no more than a month and six days when someone took a spoon and dug a hole in the wall 5 inmates escape through, all the way to the parking lot, after that the correctional officer stated that hardcore New Mexico inmates cannot be house there was another incident that occurred after the shipping of 300 inmates at Dallas county Jail it was about 45 of us inside of a Pod me, Daniel Lacy, also Andrew Miller, shitty Smitty, Kevin Smith, there was another inmate this inmate was called monkey do! And Doc Andrew Miller and me, called Chwsh while we were playing Domino's we noticed when we looked up to the glass window for the correction officers had let open the side door to the next Pod over Dallas County Jail inmates mixed in with New Mexico inmates also the second time. For about 2 hours before they decide to let them go back through the door well Monkey do see a young man urinating at the piss Style and said, to us all! Man" that guy is one sexy dude! I really like this dude. Monkey do walk over to the piss Style while Kevin was pissing and said you are really sexy! Kevin turned around and said I'm not like that somehow! That triggered monkey does to go back and said, what did you say? Kevin said, I told you I am not that way" Monkey do hit him in his face, hit him on his chin, hit him in his stomach and hit him one more time across his head and knocked Kevin out cold. Then monkey do grab his pants and start rolling them down, stating pot of gold! Pot of gold! Butt nugget! as he, started taking off his clothing while he laying on top of him tying to have sex with Kevin I said, to Daniel Lacy I'm not going to watch this!

Monkey do' stop it" right now, Monkey do' said this does not concern you Chwsh; I'm taking his Tootsie roll" not yours! I came around Monkey do' I was waiting on him to see if he was going to act a fool" thinking to myself that he cannot whip all 45 of us and if he thought he could do it he would have as I prayed silently saying please let not this man violate this young man. so Monkey do' said alright, this is just for now but not for later! He left Kevin down with his pants pulled down to his knees we help him to the floor and pulled his pants back up. I had received a new trial for my actual conviction under Attorney Darryl Brochure in 1996 and I got shipped to Dallas County Jail illegally so we filed a writ of habeas corpus, but in the process two inmates didn't agree! Doc Andrew Miller did not agree the way Robert More named one eye, that he's filing our cases jointly and they will be dismissed all together with prejudice we should done them separately but it got dismissed with prejudice because we joining them all together it was a sad month we were at the county Jail for one month and a week then they shipped us back but we went to Central New Mexico. After we arrived there to Central B Pod, I was in room 135 Lacy was in room 134 we were both in the room for no more than 25 minutes then about 23 people bum rush in to Lacy's room as I ran out of my room pushing between them to get inside Lacy room they were all pressed up against him, telling him you are a dead man I said, gentlemen, gentlemen" what's going on? Gilbert Serna and Jake's Chaves where the head speakers of the meeting and he said, you can leave Chwsh you don't have nothing to do with this! Our gangs know all about you, and how you're allied with all" so know means with you, but only honesty! with Chwsh. We've been waiting on Lacy for 11 years so they disparage and went out of the room rejoicing with their first balled up in the air saying that we finally got Mayte. Meaning slang, for Man it is black beetle, true meaning" we finally got him, been a long waiting for 11 years and Karma has destined for him to come right back here! History about the Pod' was constantly black males was put into the Pod and Mexican men and Spanish clicks that wanted to graduate into being a gangster "we will have to answered, to one friend but if he chooses the wrong way "while they whatever variety they would drop devices on top of them giving the black males concussion head broken, stabbings kicking them until they're out unconscious. Some of the inmates got their cells burnouts year after year! week after week everyone was scared to come inside the Pod with me and Lacy was. I asked Lacy what's going on what happened? I had a few run-ins with their friends not too long ago and I got the best of them Chwsh you have no part of this you're innocent! you don't have to be in the middle of this, besides your supporters, and alliances I'm good as dead anyways happen to you. What is this, Lacy? So I see this is when my flesh supposed to be a Chameleon right! I would not stand by and watch my brother die in front me never" there were two most important, to get these B.F.L stop them from making it to Houston T, that's done! And over the other you Lacy you have to stop the change getting back in here! The rest I can Live with" then Lacy said to me, listen Chwsh! History I have been charged 11 years a rape case in one of the females in kin to all these people they fought me the first time and I beat them all I will give them a hell of a fight but I won't be able to make it through this time Chwsh would you give this letter to my ex-wife, and my brothers most of all my daughter, too many enemies. You have already written a letter, so you knew about this you didn't tell me then I said, enough! Of that' say no more! You're going to give that letter to your family yourself, you will get out of this prison a change must come, if they want war then war, we give them. The next morning they came running back to the room in the Pod door open where everybody came into the room not only the 15 people but additional 20 the correctional officer in the high tower just looked at us and pop the locks to where other inmates came straight into the side door. But I know that they were not Sanchez people, and they were not Latin kings. an inmate's words were that they were want to be S.N.M rejects from all gangs, they came towards us, and stated, I told you to leave but since you're not going to leave then both of y'all will die! Are the easy way-out P.C. Like true warriors you are. I tap Lacy on the leg and say okay we'll P.C. Meaning we will gladly walk into protective custody on our own, I asked what time can we do this? They said 12 noon tomorrow okay deal. we left out of Lacy room and went to the yard and ask everybody out there! Only been here 2 days can I get some metal, from anyone out here everybody was quiet again, I said, I'm going to war me and Lacy tomorrow morning can I get a shank. since they wouldn't say anything, I started walking looking at the ground to the sand and noticed a string hanging out of the sand. a yarn thread I pulled on it and a large piece of metal came out and I put it inside my right boot and I got one more of them and I put it inside my left boot then walk through the metal detector and went back to the Pod B Lacy followed after me. before entering B Pod a correctional officer came out, and looked at me and Lacy and stated you again! While looking at Lacy is this your second time coming back? Y'all need to arm yourselves for tomorrow morning there's no changing that could be brought" I said but you are the correction officer right? listen don't get smart with me; I'm giving a warning they coming for you guys. as I left the presence of the officer that was stand at the door, and went into the Pod, I said, to myself" I know you giving me a warning but looks like you should be able to do something, being a correctional officer. The next morning arrived 12:00 noon I was watching TV and the whole Pod filled up with inmates entered in as they filled up B Pod, I asked everybody who don't want us to be inside this Pod. Make it known right now for the last time. Nobody didn't say nothing' going once! going twice! I knew all their people were not there! Gilbert Serna was there! Jake Chaves was there but nobody else! Other people that supported them was not there. I post up at my door all night waiting patiently finally first in the morning after noon came at 1:00 p.m. I went in the room fell down on my knees and start praying please quash Abb give us knowledge to overcome these wicked intentions with the spirit of righteousness and knowledge to not kill but to usher and make a change of the environment in this Pod justice peace everyone in being united together and love each other but in this wretched area where we as inmates refusing to allow to be govern and rule with respect and compassion towards one another" after Lacy enter my room, I told him do not kill nobody make them bleed but no killing Chwsh! They've been after me, for 11 years and you want me to let them live? And they will keep on trying to kill me, us I said, Lacy gives me your word you won't kill nobody? After 30 seconds of Lacy staring directly into my eyes; okay Chwsh I give you my word I won't kill no one time we left my room I went into the Lounge to sit and watch TV later I heard a commotion Jake Travis was upstairs arguing with Lacy I ran upstairs before I could see what's up Lacy swing and broke Jake nose and was beating him as Gilbert Serna came running up to me with a knife I stabbed him with his own knife first in his lower stomach nothing critical and was pistol-whipping him hitting Serna over again with my fist holding the knife in my right hand, telling him to stay his grounds and that's all you'll get, stay your grounds as as I turned, around I slipped down in his blood, and rolled over got back up and started going to each room pulling on the door knobs trying to get it open blood was on the door knob inmates yelling at me from behind the door I had nothing to do with it please! I had nothing to do with that Serna, I went to the next room, trying to open his cell block door but he yells out I'm from the state of Texas H-Town and I said to him you allowing your own brothers to be eliminated with no help. So I couldn't get into his room I wanted to get into that room worser then all the other's it is amazing how everybody right now saying that they're from the state of Texas I went to the next room and to the next room I hate putting on the suit of a serpent because when you come to this boiling point you want to eliminate all odds of the possibilities of somebody coming to get you. I had blood on every door knob finally LT. Major white came into B Pod and walking upstairs quickly Lacy looked up at me and said, Chwsh! Chwsh! Major white as I saw Major white coming up the stairs where the army full of correctional officers' electrical shields. I rolled over again on the floor, in Gilbert Serna's blood laid down prostrated as though I was hit, looked up and said they got me man! Holding my side as they put me in a stretcher carried me out of B Pod through the doors. Finally the C.O.s knew what was up! They ran out the door yelling to the correctional officer Hey! Hey! He's the one who's doing the sticking he is the one that's doing the sticking quickly get him! As I got up off the stretcher running towards the recreation yard, a whole yard of inmates looks like if they were in a riot" looking towards me with their hands on the fence and saying throw the shank on the roof? Chwsh as I slowed down from running, two corrections officers and one large heavy set black women got closer and closer telling me slow down baby hey slow down so the next minute I realize she dove on top of me with her breasts on my head saying look at these!Down baby easy, easy, easy kept shoving her breast to my face. Now I'm back at the hard time seg unit and Major white stated are you going to tell me what's going on, are you wants to be a gangster? LT Major white replied okay' then who is this, Daniel Lacy? I don't know who Daniel Lacy is! I done this all by myself. so immediately they ship Daniel back to Las Cruces why I stayed in seg for 90 days Major white had come back and said that was a good thing that you call a Pod meeting and because of you doing this' you were just simply protecting your own. And Chwsh, don't play me as another C.O. LT, I know you saved, plenty of lives all those officers would have lost their live if it wasn't for what you did" at the P.N.M north unit and believe me I will tell every officer when you leave what you did now here! This what I can make happen. I will drop the two shanks charges of 9 years a piece, for the two knives you got caught with. You will be here for 90 days with no good time, one more thing? Who was the officer that warned you, to get a knife! Give me a name" I need to know who he is! I can't do that he did save me even though I was strapping down with some iron anyway. One morning a correction officer brought an inmate to my room warm-hearted person name Rodney county that was in the general population went directly to seg just to be lock up to meet me to give me his radio before he leaves within one week from now. And he said to me we only known you guys for two days but you guys handled for us that we couldn't do for eight years. Hey! Everybody is sad that you and Lacy went to war and nobody help you guys out this radio is my only possession I can give this! And is all I have I hope it gives you strength and for what you've done for us man we got a peace on this compound even with correctional officers we need more people just like you and Lacy I act like I was going to hit! Somebody and correctional officer locked me up! I came here to seg just to give you this radio Truly you are R.C.F.F. Our heroes I said thank you I know now that you are genuine as they come, no black person other than the crew that I'm with are the people that I find grace and mercy that the

Lord has shined a light for people to be righteousness and respectful to me have never given me anything in here only the Lord who I serve but beyond that no brother it would be very appreciate. Later that night I went into a deep vision, sleeping heavily noticing I was getting ready to eat some food and it was a form of bacteria growing like worms in it I seen the vision of me eating something and it played a part of me being in the hospital possibly death. That following morning they let Gilbert Serna get out of his cell and serve us trays to eat but word was he put his medication are drugs inside my food to poison me as Gilbert came to my door the cop undone the porthole, I slung the tray at Gilbert Serna and I hit him on his face. They made Serna get back into his room and after my 90 days was over with between the time counting down of my 90 days of seg the warden of Central correction facility allow them to have a get together" of eating out and recreation out on the yard as a family reunion everyone started sending food to my room to make sure I have plenty of food to eat then as usual when things get back to the normal of enjoying yourselves more than an hour or two there's always a change of environment they shipped me back to Las Cruces I had to go to the infirmary to be seen by a dentist for my tooth the doctor comes up and tells me that I need to slip into a gown and lay down on the table I said sir! I'm coming here for a tooth and for my eyes to be checked and to see if I need a pair of eye glasses. Take off your clothes the doctor told me. I said sir I am not taking off my clothes I'm here for a tooth problem! And for an eye glasses shut up! And quit being disgruntle and I spoke get me out of here! I never was seen went back to the Pod about two months later I decided to go to the gym, went by Lacy room to pick him up as we walked over to the gym Lacy was agitated with me on my character and finally, he told me how is it' that I get shipped away from Central and you stay there somebody tells me that there's been some. Kind of sell out with his fist balled looking straight at me in anger. I said that's true there has been. If you want to hit me, hit me! You are the only fleshy brother out here that I believe in, and trust in so naturally my best friend can hit me" remember let me give you some input I sold myself out to get you back to the Las Cruces why I stayed inside hard seg 90 days they let Gilbert Serna out the one that I took care of he tried to poison my food and I know that for a fact that the Lord is giving me a vision so I didn't want to eat that morning and I threw it at his face he was being a special inmate with privileges well anyway I told Major white I don't know Daniel Lacy you already told me you've been in for 15 years straight. I didn't want you to pick up another 9 years charge you didn't have a metal shank I did. And pick up another 9 years charge for second shank you didn't have a metal shank the only way to get you out of there no more years added to your time, was for you to get out to see your daughter you telling me about all the time big carry is around your daughter taking my daughter for granted, sexing her playing mind games. you said he's your best friend I need to help her" Lacy stated very loudly I'm sorry I will whoop that person ass, for telling me lies. I said no you're not that defeats my purpose of looking out for you don't do that please! Praise in yachwshuah let's keep working hard and get out of this prison stop the chain. Several days later there were certain individuals wanted me to be the treasurer of the black awareness group so I became the treasure everyone voted for me and Jesse Wright was the president of the black awareness group. my job was to hold all the money and to sell pastries donuts, order sheet cakes ,cheese cakes, different varieties of pies along with 15 dozen donuts we were a very prosperous group and making money we had more money on the compound than anybody. One day the present decided to come in my room and say give me a dozen of donuts without me paying for it no sir! Not unless you pay me for it. Can't do that' did you hear what I told you I'm not asking you I'm going to take it from you, Jesse right replied. I said it is true you have never lost a fight" but you will lose one if you oppose this to me again in a threatening manner" now all this is the cause of donuts? Really wow! But we do have extra donuts and I'm going to slide you as many as possible now the next time you come in my room making demands I will push that imaginary bird that's on your shoulder and I will take that imaginary coffee that you keep drinking every morning and holding it in your right hand I will spill it all on your shirt! Jesse wright okay! so where is my donuts? I said underneath your bed where you hide the rest of them that came off the truck. Jessie wright came back to the room and apologized with a hug and said forgive me it's all good Jesse I got your back. We tried to show the whole penitentiaries how the black awareness group should be ran, the first thing we did locate every black male in lock up hard time seg. called for Lieutenant Delatorre gave him and his staff two dozen of donuts and ask permission to bring to lock up to give every inmate donut in seg also to exchange messed up clothes that they had and was tore up, gave them brand-new warm-ups sweat suits and shoes gave Chills Roswell his people four dozen of donuts gave Sanchez his people four dozen of donuts but the rest of the donuts have to be sold through the concession stand and everybody was so happy to buy the donuts also it may order sheet cakes cheese cakes with everything on it we got it but later became a problem with the Texas Syndicate and one Latin king inmate they both had a family member that died in the free world and he had no way of being able to go to the funeral I talk to the group and everybody said no! Don't give anyone money to help out so I stated it looks like I need to go ahead and leave this black awareness group because if I can't be who I am behind this righteous cause! and give to the people and spread peace then what's the purpose of even being a treasurer? Only the groups personal treasurer but nobody else! Later that following morning as I was returning back to give up my rights as being treasurer everyone there said, if you think it's a righteous reason then you can and go ahead, we don't support it but we do support you! Fine and I took care of that so I gave the Latin king $900.00 and a Texas Syndicate $900.00 they were able to go and see their family member get buried. We have an account over $7800 and if we get shipped for any reason the money is the warden regardless. And so all the work we do and giving out to anyone in need we still lose in long run because our account will be zero balance when we come back so this time we making sure that everybody did receive whatever they needed before we leave Las Cruces and when they came back warden found out and had a problem with what I did. Word reached from a very reliable source that they are looking for blood shed, and fights not peace and love everyone didn't understand that but they knew it came directly from the actual source Chuck. Now to pass by time we always play poker Jesse Wright history about Jesse, was the man who was getting ready to fight Mike Tyson with a pet bird named Tweety it's always on his left arm but you can't see him drinking a hot cup of coffee, burning his lips but no coffee inside the cup. And no cup in his hand. I had a small straight flush to Jesse White boat! Kings over jacks, nobody really talk to Jesse because they were scared to getting punched out and since I was winning and I know he couldn't beat my hand I gave my hand up! By saying I got show rock in my hand, straight flush to Jesse just tells me the truth" so I said, Jesse what was the reason you came in the penitentiary you tell me the truth! And I know it's the truth I give the $197.00 that is one hundred and ninety-seven dollars to you that's is what all this stuff worth you have your hot pot; you put in the game! You have your stinger back you put in and your coffee pot, you have warm ups suits, you have canteen that will last you for 2 months and this poker game" Jesse Wright said alright Chwsh! I tell you and the pot of money and canteen it's all mine! I was high' on crack! Inside of a pawnshop stealing Ak-47s dancing with a pink teddy bear" where they get the movie called colors that was actually me on the movie of colors dancing with the pink teddy bear they got that thought of doing that from me, I said yeah right! I don't know about that, Jesse said I'm telling you the truth I've been locked up for 16 straight years as we heard doors open correctional officers came down the tower ran up to our poker table and slammed down the news paper clip, in front of the table saying I told you all along that was you! In this news paper clip we can barely see the picture but we knew it was you correctional officers started laughing over and over again even us, at the table was laughing over and over because we remember the guy on the movie called colors dancing with a pink teddy bear now I know why Jesse White is so fascinated with pink teddy bears he sell envelopes with a pink teddy bear on the end of them. We laughed all the way to seg all to hard lock up! Then I went to Santa Rosa where the year came for correctional officer Ralph Garcia to lose his life. May the Lord have mercy on his soul, which really should not happen to him at all, neither to any correctional officer for the women was the actual person they really wanted also two more correctional officers two days prior to this Major incident before this happened. The one that was bringing the drugs into Santa Rosa but then changed his mind and said no. one day after lunch we were all sitting down when the 18th street Leader Diablo start speaking on issues drugs money a correctional officer refusing to bring in the goods he better bring it in, if not I have a problem, if he doesn't there will be a problem! Mousie and the rest of the 18th Street gang started asking me questions about the bible at this moment in time they were peace no arguments no fighting everybody was one on one accord. Then some started talking hey! did you hear about the movie the longest yard Burt Reynolds is in the movie he's making a second one at the Santa Fe Main correctional facility others speaking of Snoop Dogg supposed to be in the movie some say Nelly is Snoop Dogg's cousin, I will let all of you know on what I see and Valentino when we go out in a few weeks from now, we will see if they're making a movie or not. It would be nice to get some help in here then one of the 18th St. youngsters named Reyes said what do need help with Chwsh we got everything in control. I said, no you don't you're out of control get the Lord in your life they didn't as anything to me just smiled as we kept on playing dominoes. For the first time they were at peace for almost 2 weeks we started playing more pinochle games and dominoes and then a man by the name of Monkey does' moves into the Pod at the same time we started back playing poker and I have always won every poker game. The following day my friend KD said Hey! Chwsh why don't you let Monkey do' come and play with us! In poker you scared you might have a little competition I said, you don't know who you're playing with Monkey do' is not, who you think her is don't talk about him KD said he's a good person. Chwsh he really is a good person and what do you mean? Hey! Alright I will call him over to play poker with us, so I called Monkey do' over to play poker! So I walked over to his room and said Hey! Monkey do' how are you doing? Would you like to play poker with us? Everybody pitches in canteen commissary and that's about it! we play for no more no less, that's great! I'm good with that as we were playing cards there were four of us, KD, Alan, Valentino, and me we all noticed that Monkey do' kept staring upstairs looking at a particular person later Monkey do' said hold up! He went upstairs and start talking to an Indian boy name Robert Soshee everyone notice we always had to wait for him, but later on the officer came and noticed that nobody wouldn't play cards, he noticed that Monkey do' was in his room with Sohee they're now roommates later on KD and Alan came to me and Valentino and said Chwsh what's going on with Monkey do? I said to KD and Alan listen this man is known for taking people butt and if you guys lose in poker and you owe him he's taking it" Ooh, hell no! KD and Alan said you're right Chwsh he's a sick individual I will fight to end. we had to go back to our cell at 7:15 lock down they stayed in their cell for one hour extra we come back out, but they both stayed in their cell Monkey do' refuses to leave. Correctional officer came by his cell and looked in and thought that Monkey do' and Sohee had a lover's spat, seen Monkey do' on top of Sohee butt. And so the correctional officer does room checks at 2:30 they came back around and seen Monkey do' still, on top of Soshee butt. This time they notice that Soshee hands was tied up! With a sheet and his legs was tied up! with a sheet and seeing Monkey do' had a razor blade in his mouth, on top of him, telling him to shut up! also Soshee had a sheet that was around his head covering his mouth to keep him quiet while Monkey do' forced himself, on top of him and proceeded to have sex with him and raped him correction officers broke into his door pulling Monkey do' off of Soshee but he wouldn't get off of him. Monkey do' was immediately taken to Bernalillo County for resentencing to add to 25 years for 18 more years so his actual sentence was enhanced two counts of six penetration charges of rape the whole floor was locked down for weeks. after 3 weeks of of locked down, correctional officer came to me and said, you need to see your case manager a phone call from someone very importance to you. Who what is about" I don't know Chwsh talk to your case manager" Alicia C Tafoya. As I arrived to case manager office, I ask anybody home! And she said Hey my friend" Ooh I know you didn't hell no! Alicia, hell yeah! Here Chwsh she got up walked around her desk and gave me a hug and use my phone call back now I started dialing the phone number she gave me and man answered, and said Hey! Boy this is your dad! we've been looking everywhere for you, I hired a detective and they traced your social security number#

to Santa Fe main facility but about time I tried to make some arrangements you were gone. Yeah, dad sorry I these charges on my dad over told me, boy I don't give a about your charges you are my son and I know Richard Johnson" well I guess I don't have to waste no more money on these Attorneys. I said no dad I'm right here! When you were calling at the main Santa Fe correctional facility hell in a fight for my life' what you mean you're in the fight for your life! Dad, I think my time is running out! Alicia said, quickly no you are not keep talking to dad you haven't heard from him in 40 years go! Chwsh my dad said who is the sweet voice next to Richard, you it like that" no dad I don't anyway while I was at the main this group called the black family leaders want to see rappers from housing T dead. There called B.F.L. They stated were going to Housing T, in months from time they will get out, but I managed to beat there ass everywhere I went, even all gangsters were making sure they didn't succeed all gangs united to eliminate them, even wardens of every correctional facility helped me out when they found out I got jumped and made me where the name of their enemies and my dad said, who were the name Z Th Ke that is crazy! Just to let you know have you heard a song called want to be a baller" yes dad I love it" that is all my brothers' children on the song! That is all your kinfolks. And your uncle James still living there! Also with you Anit Hellen's dad Alicia, say it's time man thanks you for finding me dad last words we will talk again! Dad loves you by. I was sorry, so hurt, for my dad have to hear me from this place. All this time fighting standing for my favorite Icon stars, I love all my rappers of housing T from the least to the great" Alicia you have giving more then I could beg for tears, dropping down face. my case manager said give me another hug I have another but it will be later" now get out my office Chwsh I left my case manager with the two correctional officers escorting me to my room.

Part 4

Righteous Seeds Planted

In the year 1999/09/31 one day at Santa Rosa as I was placing my literature and writing on the table, I was studying Hebrew. all the 18th Street gangsters we're all around me asking question I was letting them know that you are a Royal generation acknowledge, who you are! And let it take right or the enemy will come and take ripe and your vessels and ride you like a brand-new car then one of the members of the gang named Mousie had asked me why is Simon Peter. Also Mousie said Chwsh could you put it in layman terms I said Simon is not a name it is a tribe: Simon Shawn a fire of the people at the time of the eye. Fire ash- people-am time -w also meaning owl n-eye or king. And remember of the 12 tribes of Israel, so if you have 12 tribes, you have 12 Patriarchs of the 12 gates of the 12 cities of the 12 princess now, of the 12 Apostles but it keep being only 11 letting you know that no matter how many people you have with you there is always one deceiver" Mousie said, to me can we study every day and learn this day by day I asked Mousie can you hold the spirit of the Lord in your vessel that long. I said, that because 18th street has been known for beating, or even killing inmates 2 out of a month and if so, much not killing them, severely beating down other words can you stop what you're doing? Mousie looked at me very puzzled as I walked away. Now one day me and my friend Valentino Garcia, I was talking about the word at the table before long we went up, to the room I braided his hair about eight cornrows was hanging seven inches of hang time I had finished braiding Valentino hair he stood up! And Val, was walking down the steps Diablo 18th street Leader came up, and said who braided this white boy's hair? Valentino was Spanish not white Mexican gangsters don't get along with Spanish gangsters are you don't really have to be a gangster just be a regular inmate with long braids I told Diablo I did as he got little bit closer, I said, looks like you got a little gene in yourself, I said that because it was very strong rumors that Diablo was part black, part Mexican. Diablo cuts his hair completely bald he don't want no one to know that he's part black. At least that's what the rumor was and why I stated it later Diablo call a meeting to E Pod all his 18-street gang were circled all around him as we set away on the other side listening to him, he was talking very low but we knew what he was talking about looks like we got kill one of our own, then we can initiate the riot. And get as many Chesterses baby rapers pedophiles, as possible and including snitches, that correctional officer has stopped our drugs from coming in we're not taking this no money y'all guys will go to recreation make it to the gym and why they playing basketball you will cause a scuffle to plan of which one of our own who you are going to stick, in the head after he dies, they would know that this is not a race war. after that everybody should be running out of the gym and everybody will be coming back to E Pod and then we will grab that cop, the correctional officer who was telling us don't run a thing! I am not' and no longer bringing drugs into this place for you low life bastards and that C.O. Will be second on the list we will have fun with her, then at that time we will barricade the door with both Coca-Cola machines, and take out of the machine we will strip, the insides to get metal knives, and sharpen them we should be ready for anyone who comes to this door, if they can't get through the door, one said, how are we going to get the women to come in? Whoever is coming back from the gym after we do what we say we're going to do inside the gym, then whoever outside coming in, grab her throw her into E Pod along with that correctional officer who's refusing to bring in the drugs, like he been doing. he will be here as usual because he did state after tomorrow, he said, it was his last day working for our location. Diablo finish. Everybody was laughing thought it was a joke it was about 7:30 p.m. Before the next morning of the murder of Ralph Garcia took place when me and Valentino decided to go ahead and go to the cages on the outside for our recreation 30 minutes instead of going to the gym 1 hour and half then later we will go by the law library to make our copies for our extra hour before we leave, we knew that there was going to be a change of things. Drama inside the gym for tomorrow we stared reminiscing over things of the old main facility. At the Santa Fe correctional facility where they have shut down the entire unit permanently for too many riots too many killings a correctional officer women tried to rescue her inmate boyfriend, landed in the middle of recreation yard took back to air ran out of few now she's facing 18 years in prison, that 4 years before I arrived at the main. And murders that had taken place at the old main facility. Also the findings of a stun guns dated back in 1978 ammunition two smith and western guns, underground tunnel leading all the way under the parking lot so yes, it is true the longest yard movie is being made at the facility right at this second as I walked over to the fence I could see three individuals possibly four I could've made it out to be a rapper named Nelly I couldn't make out what was in his hand he kept swinging something in his hand they noticed us and started walking real slowly towards us towards the fence as they walk closer and closer to us until the helicopters near our side gave us a warning of causing distraction by putting our hands towards the fence looking directly towards them some what a warning that's the farthest we could go I seen them staring directly at us and as I was looking at them with my long beard hanging 8 inches I said in my heart if they only knew! Standing near the fence definitely they would be very supportive for us and eager to go the right source of authorities to bring knowledge on what's about to happen to cause fire to these whole twisted games of this correctional facility Santa Rosa they would look into what's going on here at Santa Rosa but to keep them out of all things is the only way to show true love to my Icon stars they went through their persecution in life! Hell, it's time for us to man up and go through ours then Valentino said, didn't you tell me that you wrote a letter to Al Sharpton yes my friend I did but if you think that correctional officers going to allow that letter to get out of this wicked facility, then we're both foolish we proceeded to leave as we bag backwards up to get handcuffs then turning around facing the two correctional officers I stated if you don't have back up you better be post up get ready for war you need to call Maya Tafoya the officer replied we heard about what's going on tomorrow we know about that rumor it is not true I stated, it's going down now few minutes have I ever lied to this facility check my history I have saved plenty of correctional officers including the warden the officers replied sorry Chwsh everything is just hear say! As they escorted us leaving out of the cages going back to the gym asked to stop by the law library that's the least I can do for you and Valentino Garcia two correctional officers replied so the following morning, I went to the law library me and Valentino the second time, before I got there, I turned towards the correctional officer you still thank it's a rumor if Mr. Moya the warden find out you didn't listen to me or even informed him on this you will never have a job in this correctional facility ever again. you talk too much I said, 18th St wants that female correctional officer they push us hard against the door, of the law Library and unhand cuffed us and left our presence quick as we were studying, we heard a loud commotion as I looked out, of the door inmates were running from everywhere correctional officers were running to the gym. Two correctional officers were escorting two 18th Street inmates coming out of the gym and I asked the inmates what happened inside the gym? I don't know they stuck! Mousie! Mousie! He's 18th Street we don't know why they stuck Mousie as me and Valentino were walking in approaching the Pod we could feel the tension I said do you feel that he said yes something is going terribly wrong me and Val approached E Pod there was a women correctional officer outside the door I said to her do not get too close to the door get back up, I can see all eyes on us two as me and Val came walking through passing by Mr. Ralph Garcia as he was saying lock down, lock down, everybody goes in your rooms. I was approached by Diablo what did that she say? She told me lock down lock down to me and Valthen Diablo said is Mousie dead? I said he got stuck in the head I told Diablo that because I was coming from the Law Library and that's what one of the young men of 18th Street had told me that Mousie got stuck in the head and went to infirmary Diablo stated so you're telling me that he is not dead I said no! He's not are you sure he's not dead no I'm positive he's not. Then one of the 18th St. Reyes came running up to Diablo and said that lock the fucking door and now we can't get to the gym" that! Fucked our plan up! But she locked her own cop inside with us but he's not the C.O. We wanted who was talk all that bull shit! Saying he's not bringing in the Chiva no more! it we will make an example of Ralph let's get him. I heard them, but didn't turn around to see yet, I walk over to my friend named K.D and to the other standing with K.D. And started explaining to them what transpired at the gym, he took off running, now the other one person that was on side of K.D. I was explaining to him but then he took off and running as I turned around, I saw Ralph Garcia already in the door standing in front of the door, with three Shanks in him, the door open he tried to run towards the door, hands placed on the door turned and looked at the door but the women shut the door he knew he was in for a battle Ralph Garcia had his hands out he stated listen I won't tell nobody Diablo said you got all these knives in you and you telling us that you won't tell nobody Diablo came from beneath the stairs with a long piece of metal that looked like Samurai sword and shoved it through Ralph Garcia chest, as he fell backwards straight to the floor, as I was looking at Diablo on top of him, holding the shank with his right hand going down plunged it through his chest three times one of the 18th St. Reyes came up, to Diablo and said you're killing him! you're killing him! Diablo yeah! what do you think I'm trying to do? And I hope they don't like it! Let them all come to this door everybody then Diablo and Reyes and the rest of the 18th St. grabbed the Coca-Cola machines and push it against the door to barricaded, therefore nobody couldn't get inside all inmates had scattered running towards their rooms the lights were cut off permanently the correctional officers came in with about 8 to 9 other corrections officers came to pull Ralph Garcia out of E Pod before coming back with electrical Shields pr-24 nightsticks throwing tear gas bottles, inside the rooms rolling them underneath the door they rolled one underneath my door, I quickly grabbed my sock put it in the toilet grab it soak it in water and put it around my nose, and my mouth, as my hands were raised high. Correctional officers yelling at me from the front door on the floor! on the floor! hands on top of your head. a red beam of light shining on me from the window from a helicopter finally what looked like a swat team of correctional officers came through my door with the gas mask handcuff me and my Celly that refused to get down because he didn't know what they were talking about and the more he refused to the more I got maced. finally they grabbed us and hurried us down the stairs, down to a huge dark room with no lights no nothing set in the chair with then within 15 seconds a huge light was put at my face Someone questioning me who I could not see because of the generator light was within 8 ft away towards my face, he said, who killed Ralph Garcia, who killed Ralph Garcia, I think you did. you kill Ralph Garcia yes! you did! you kill Ralph Garcia that's why you're getting ready to take an airplane trip! All of y'all as I started getting weak and dizzy from the mace from the beating from the pushing shoving my face to the concrete I dozed out I don't know where I was besides being on an airplane getting shipped to Big Stone City Virginia only three of these facilities in the entire United States supermax well as we departed from Santa Rosa correctional Facility after the murder of Ralph Garcia that brought change, we boarded the airplane in white thermal suits, thin like paper nude underneath, chain on ankles and hands officers on side, handcuffed after 3 hours we arrived to Big Stone City Gap as we all single file line lining up like an

army lining up to go to war" the correctional officers of Big Stone City
Gap came out and started with us saying we hung you yesterday. I know
you were already dead we killed you yesterday that damn! Man keeps
coming back inmates Coody Jackson said, no sir! This is my first time
here! The correctional officer stated we keep killing them and killing
them and they keep coming back Coody lean towards me and said,
Chwsh I don't know what he's talking about I swear I've never been
here before! As I stared at Coody with a no answer face knowing that
the correctional officers were playing on our emotions and our feelings
so I gave Coody no reply! as with my game face on as we entered the
infirmary. They checked us out most of us already had been maced all
down our throats and swallowed it, hitting us in our chest and beat
down by two officers one officer on our left and one officer on the
right, they started telling me did you kill Ralph Garcia I'm going to go
up your butt. I'm going to go up your butt and you won't know what
hit you. I need to know now who killed Ralph the C.O. Officer said hit
him, with the taser! 50.000 volts taser and then both of the officers put
both tasers resting on each side of my shoulder watching K.D. Get
shocked with the 50.000 volts I fell asleep and next minute I woke up
on a chair that reclines backwards in the infirmary jack up! As I was
jackknife from my feet to my head downwards and a man was coming
between me saying I told you I'm going up in you I'm going up in you,
and won't feel a thing or probably you felt it before. I said, enough
you're not going to go up in me I am not that way you are not going to
do this to me I'm a human being and better known as Chwsh the
correctional officer took off his name plate and put it in his top left
pocket. And then looked at me and said who in the hell is this! darky
talking to, I looked into the air and the ceiling to the roof, and call
upon Al yachwshuah give me strength! give me patience, give me favor,
give me help give me your fleshly image then a certain calm and peace
came over me my presence of my body. An infirmary lady named Mary
Beth had showed up on the scene stood in front of me, that works with
inmates stayed on the person that was interrogating me not leaving the
officer alone with me Ms. Mary stayed with me the correctional officer
said just because your kinfolk is the warden of the facility that does not

give you the right to question me who and what I say, and what I do I'm telling you right now leave him alone, so they let me go they drop me I went down to the bunk falling to the floor being inside the infirmary, Mary Beth that's her name she took me to the shower and she washed my whole body and soak me down into the inside of a wheelchair afterwards she looked out after me when I went into a room Ms. Mary said I don't think they were trying to go up in you and violate you they were trying to see if you keister any drugs. By the way I hope you feel clean it's the best I could do most likely you will be going to a Pod to a room at the end of the two days are three later I left went into a Pod and the officer had red lines all over the entire area and we had to sign paperwork that" what bullet we would like to be shot with real bullet, bean bags, or mylar tubular, I said neither one of the officers escorting me to my cell. At that time one inmate accidentally stepped over the red line and the rifle point outside the glass window shot the young man and then said, gosh! I forgot to shoot him with the beanbag we were locked down for 3 hours before we were able to come back out, we are in the highest level of a supermax only three in the united stated people that's on death row and that's dying and doing life years lethal injection because no one here getting out in 2 years but only New Mexico inmates being at a supermax level 3 one day as we were walking going to the chow hall some extra inmates was walking in front of us and they walked all the way up to us and said where are y'all guys from we stood at the high tower and look back at him with our hands held high he said why are you not saying nothing where are y'all guys coming from a loud voice on a speaker saying you got 5 seconds to move he quickly move back and raise his hands up and left the area quickly we also heard that the New York governors found out what happened to us in getting shipped so they offer to help us they started working from New York to help us get back to our jurisdiction once Big Stone city Virginia I will say for the record either John Shanks are the person that had the position of power secretly ship, not only 205 inmates' people from Santa Rosa. But they shipped every bad boy characteristic that they can ship! they put them all in the loop Las Cruces people had nothing to do with Santa Rosa, Central had nothing to do with what happened as Santa Rosa, the P.M. North had thing to do with the riot also Lee Roy Torres nothing to with Santa Rosa but he did kick off the riot in Las cruces 1996 and pushed a weight bar through the head of a black man and had his gang 300 hundred essay against 15 fifteen black men but are in 1999, chills from Roswell had nothing to do with it every person from every are of Albuquerque in prison got a taste of Big Stone city Gap and when the prison guard at the supermax Virginia correctional officers found out that we were getting out within 2 years from the supermax prison they could not hold no power over us we cross over the red lines they no longer could shoot us so therefore they had no alternatives but to send us 205 inmates back to Santa Rosa every inmate that had a sexual crime got put into an experimentation registration sex offender Program by Fitzgerald Andrea head clinician two master degrees and made me a mentor over 25 people she was very happy to hear the knowledge of the bible of God, and the people are black and the Romans are Latin white men and the Greek are of Alexander the Great and the Jewish people that is put their have created a anti juice foundation, she understands all that I was saying of it! and inside this Correctional Facility. She was the bravest courageous best clinician physician psychologist ever! I went in to see my caseworker Miss Alicia discussing my good time she kept asking me to call the number hopefully when I get in touch with my mom so I would have a place to parole to instead of trying to parole to Albuquerque I had to see if mom still stayed at her area in Beaumont Texas 1928 Delaware street, Alicia been doing skip tracing for me she gave me a piece of paper and said here! I said, you mean to tell me out of all these years at 12 years you telling me that you found the number just call it! and see that all you can do caseworker" Alicia Tafoya I was also explaining it to my caseworker that my 550 days from county jail was never applied to my computation of my sentence. She said but remember it was me that notarized you're 17 books of the Bible already written in Hebrew okay you're right! Alicia then said, I know Richard I'm not trying to hold you back from getting out" Alicia stated and by looking at all the good time that was restored. you should be out since 2002 they done it at the wrong time maybe you can call your Attorney Paul Livingston and tell him you should have been out since 2002 I'm sorry Richard but the only person that can pull this one is Morya our actual warden is you might be able to write Mr. John Shanks but there is nothing, I can do sorry still my time was drawing near because if I wasn't out, then I'm just burning my time in finishing where I won't have any time to do on the outside killing my number. I went in my cubicle and sat down and got right back up to go call the number over and again finally a person answered the phone appears to be my mom hello! I said, is this Emma Johnson's residence! yes, it is but my name is Emma Benoit I got married a few years back and I went ahead and came back to my house I got kicked out, by his children. And I was living with Curly Benoit then I said, no wonder I kept writing letters and it kept saying returned to the sender with the finger on it yeah because I just moved back in his children are grown, they knew the Curly gave me the power of Attorney and making me the final decisions to his affairs. I was married for 10 years and currently he told me to take out insurance policy because he knew the time was drawing near for him to die. Curly asked me to be power of Attorney over his affairs including the insurance policy which I paid out of my money and when he passed the children got mercy funeral home to take care of the affairs and take the money and that's why I'm here back in the house I see do you know who this is? This sounds like Leo! Leslie! I said no this no this is Richard boy! where have you been? In prison and Big A, found out, he managed to called me and the person that was with him contact me a year ago! he knew where I was are you sure this is Richard my son what's your social security 4#015#### yeah this is my son which is why you had us worried about you. well Dad knew where I was! yeah but he had investigated to find out where you were! I've been locked up mom since 92/94 sentences in a county jail from 94 to 2005 I'll be getting out within 3 to 4 months from now they wanted me to be able to parole to Beaumont. And not Bernalillo County mom said, come on I need help come on back home. all right now I love you very much I love you too! Take care I'll call you again before I get out! All right bye-bye Alicia Tafoya you did it again! I' am lost for words, this was your second surprise! You have done what you said, you're going to do for me! Chwsh I will not be complete until you out of this give me my hug! The officers are looking for you now! After I was leaving caseworker, I was approached by two guards asking me are you ready early in the morning at 5:30 said my good byes gave my radio to someone that might need it gave my warm-ups clothing to any person that might need it. remembering how this change of a new class came it is inevitable of new friends since the experimentation started head clinician Andrea Fitzgerald gave me a hug and saying goodbye Rasheem, gave me a hug and spoke goodbye Kyle Allen gave me a hug and said goodbye while walking me to the front entrance of Santa Rosa Correctional Facility and along with the two officers asked me do you need blue jeans? Of course! Do you need T-shirts? Why ask me of course! Is there anything Elis you need? yes, I need that check cut ASAP to get on that bus as they walked me out to a van the weather was hot and humid day. And I stated, that I need for correctional officers here to escort me outside to take me downtown the sun was so bright it felt as though there was a new sun of a new day as I was walking holding a bag full of things which was very important to me 17 books scriptures along with my Hebrew notes and documentation and books that father Dannis has given me through the years correction officers ask hey! what's in that you want me to hold it for you? no! I got it myself, silently I prayed for the time walking out to the van Ala Yachwshuah Ala Yachwshuah the spiritual man has become all-powerful within my 13 ½ years, blending in prison I grossed over 4,700 converts' finally the parole said to me that I am ready to get out 2004 second month 18-day parole to Beaumont Texas, since I've done my time in prison I only have parole not probation, it was already killed. So I will be doing 9 months in the free world. These are my last days in prison Santa Rosa facility Sanchez came up to me. you were right about everything Chwsh I'm very happy and privileged to be around you. Now there's a word went out last week the ones we all know of, B.F.L. we stepped on and squashed the group is completely is no more! who swore to you! That they will get those Housing T, rappers come on! Chwsh after all the years they have families, and children's brothers Sanchez stated I said, please! Tell me! we believe they're coming for you today! Chwsh I'll be watching out for you I have two people that will be on the bus along with you and when you get to Bernalillo County at the bus station the greyhound bus station, I have a person in there looking for you also and make sure that you're able to hop on that bus without being delayed please! my brother' get on the first bus that's there. To leave for Texas and just to let you know you have taught me a great deal about loving my brother and my black people I know now that there's in my flesh of my flesh and bone of my bone and where I am in the Penta I will make sure that I would not war against them unless it's actually a reason behind it and would not be over race for we are as one. I arrived there at the bus station an hour and a half early so I bought something to eat at the area a small deli inside the bus station and when I sat down someone set down in the back of me still shell shocked from Penitentiary, I told the person that was sitting in the back of me you better get your ass in the front! what the hell do you think you! Oops I'm sorry I'm out of here the bus just showed up quickly ran out, gave him my ticket and hopped on it. when I managed to get a seat when I sat down on the bus someone in front of me had a pair of earphones with the music blasting saying what it is y'all what up! can a player! keep in touch, put my seat in a laid-back position meditating upon the scriptures of Isaiah finally leaving Albuquerque New Mexico 2004 second month 18th day and a six-hour. Praise hall Yachwshuah.

www.ingramcontent.com/pod-product-compliance
Lightning Source LLC
Chambersburg PA
CBHW070913100726
47907CB00008B/2312